Abel

Published by Abel Publishing

info@abelpublishing.com
www.abelpublishing.com

First published on 23 June 2008
by Abel Publishing

A CIP catalogue record for this book
is available from the British Library

Printed and bound in Great Britain by
Stanley L Hunt (Printers) Limited
Midland Road
Rushden
Northants
NN10 9UA

ISBN: 978-0-9559423-0-3

85/1000

Publisher's Statement

"If you want to build a ship, don't herd people together to collect wood and don't assign them tasks and work; but, rather, teach them to long for the endless immensity of the sea" (Antoine de Saint-Exupéry)

Abel is an artistic and literary endeavour. It is first and foremost a vessel of creativity which is still taking shape. *Abel Publishing* was registered on World Book Day 2008, although the vessel has been evolving over a number of years, for the endless immensity of oceans, seas and waters is life itself.

It seems, therefore, appropriate to launch *Abel Publishing* into unknown seas with poetry, and the novella and play 'Hell Unlimited. Where Shakespeare met Goethe'.

'Hell Unlimited' is about the way literature and art, and in particular Shakespeare and Goethe contribute to survival strategies in different camps, and the way they help to prevent an internal shipwreck for some prisoners. Shakespeare and Goethe wrote great tragedies. Yet, the tragedies of which humans are capable, and the destructive powers they unleash, are what have marked out human beings, and what have especially characterised the last century. They have also shaped the beginnings of this century. 'Hell Unlimited' transcends the historical and nightmarish framework and concludes with a glimpse of artistic unity, a sense of release, and with a beautiful vision.

It is with this vision that this vessel is launched.

ABEL PUBLISHING

Hell Unlimited

Where Shakespeare Met Goethe

J. M. McNally was born and brought up in Grimsby, attended London University and graduated with a First Class Honours in German with French, and later was also awarded a Doctor of Philosophy for 'Creative Misbehaviour' (part-published as a book in 2000). J. M. McNally was a practising language and drama teacher and senior lecturer for many years specialising in language teaching methodology and motivation, and also literary and political cabaret, and, since 1988, has also spent periods of time in Berlin. J. M McNally's academic work, including cross-cultural work and work of a historical nature, has received numerous awards and fellowships since 1987. Those who know the author, will understand why the author has mentioned these facts.

Hell Unlimited is based on documentary evidence and the author's own personal and original research into this period of history which began in 2000. *Hell Unlimited* is fictional, with the opening scene and characters first taking shape in October 2004. Any resemblance to living or deceased persons is entirely coincidental.

At the time of researching this work, the author was not aware that her relative had been imprisoned in a mining camp near Auschwitz. His story, and that of others forced to work down the mines has resulted in the non-fiction literary work *Marching without Knowing* (forthcoming).

J. M. MCNALLY

Hell Unlimited
Where Shakespeare Met Goethe

I wish to acknowledge and pay tribute to the many people with whom I've had the great honour of speaking over the years in different countries around the world, and who include survivors of the Nazi concentration camps and work camps. I also wish to pay tribute to the survivors of contemporary kinds of illegal imprisonment such as Guantánamo Bay, and contemporary kinds of unjust deportations or forcible transfers of populations and which include the citizens of the Chagos (Diego Garcia). Their indomitable spirit brightens the darkness.

Let us also not forget peoples and individuals still being subjected to intolerable conditions in camps, ghettos and illegal prisons and thrown at the mercy and whims of brutal oppressors. Such places include Gaza and Darfur. May their indomitable spirit pierce the darkness.

Thank you to all those who have helped
to make this book possible
especially my parents

If that the heavens do not their visible spirits
Send quickly down to tame these vile offences,
It will come:
Humanity must perforce prey on itself,
Like monsters of the deep

The Tragedy of King Lear, 4.2

It was on my very first day in the place that I came across Carl. Snow was silently falling and I had already been trekking around for more than three hours before I stumbled upon him in a corner of one of the barracks. Although the building was only dimly lit, I knew the figure in the shadows had to be his. His silhouette was so familiar to me. I could still trace every contour and curve of his body, and from any angle, or in any position.

Carl was talking about Shakespeare. Shakespeare was right, he was proclaiming, All the world is a stage. And this place? Even Shakespeare writing his greatest tragedy could not have imagined this world. This stage. Carl lowered his eyes, his voice, and allowed for a pregnant pause before he proceeded. His timing was still impeccable. Then he lifted his eyes, opened them wide and fixed them on a point a few metres in front of him and, in a voice that was wistful yet commanding, declared, When we are born we cry that we are come to this great stage of fools…

He had no audience. No conversation partner. He was talking to the walls. I listened for some time at a distance. It wasn't a confused monologue, it was more like a quietly despairing, yet philosophic rant with moments of silent reflection in between. Robed in dirty clothes and propped up rather awkwardly by a pile of sacks, Carl nevertheless still retained an air of dignity.

Tragic dignity. Like Time preserved in golden soot. And his voice could still be flexed and modulated to convey the greatest and gentlest of sentiments.

He was King Lear abandoned to his horrendous fate, but still capable of questioning it. Yet, for once in his life he was not acting a part. He was not playing King Lear, Hamlet or Goethe's Mephistopheles on the great stages throughout Europe and America. This imprisonment had become his world. His stage. And he was now assigned a part which he was still struggling to understand and interpret, As flies to wanton boys, are we to the gods, they kill us for their sport, he murmured. And day-by-day he still worked on it, reflected on it and tried to come to terms with it. He'd been learning this part for nearly two years by the time I arrived. He was determined to master it.

I very quickly understood that most inmates of this place had invented their own personal strategies for coping with their lives behind the guarded walls, thrown as they were at the complete mercy of their captors and well hidden from the outside world. Some were more successful than others. Carl's was to interpret this reality through Shakespeare. Perhaps, as a way of rising above what was happening? Of trying to keep in focus the wider canopy of life and death, of good and evil, of tragedy, absurdity and comedy? It was difficult to tell as I listened intently to his extended soliloquy on that bleak afternoon in January.

I sensed, however, that Carl's spirit was breaking and succumbing to the brutality of this place. To this very different kind of theatre that I still had properly to experience. I am bound upon a wheel of fire that mine own tears do scold like molten lead, sighed Carl as he clasped both hands to his head and swayed to and fro. He seemed to have witnessed so much. Perhaps he already knew too much. Carl, the great master of roles, could barely trick or train himself into playing more, I thought. Yet, he had not given up either, This feather stirs, she lives, if it be so, it is a chance which does redeem all sorrows, he suddenly announced as he slowly stooped to pick up and then gently caress a tiny feather that had been abandoned to the filth of the floor. I, by contrast, had yet to find my part.

Until now, I had only heard rumours about this place. I could choose to ignore these and, unconsciously or consciously, comply with the pretence that this place really was a safe haven. After all, many famous people from all over Europe had apparently chosen to come here. Many, especially the older ones, had sold their property and possessions in order to secure a privileged place in this part of the world. They had believed the advertisements in local newspapers.

They had hoped for a better life. I, too, had wanted to believe all this as I read about it. I had wanted to hope.

I also had not been prepared for the deception. Yet, strange as it may seem, the true nature of the place did not hit me straightaway, unlike most of my travelling companions. The welcoming blows and the snatching away of our belongings had surprised me. As had the barbed wire and guards. The delousing. The organised humiliation. But I had somehow managed to readjust my senses and bring them back into line again quite quickly. It was only now on seeing Carl that my mind began to spin uncontrollably and that my emotions began to collide in terrifying ways. It was only now that my feelings, hitherto well-contained, rushed round my head and body with alarming speed and vigour. In Carl, I suddenly perceived the whole truth about this place in an instant. In one stark image.

The great Carl had been reduced to a beggar, to a beast. Was it not Lear who grimly states, Allow not nature more than nature needs, man's life is cheap as beast's? And had not Carl uttered those very same words on the stage in Prague where I had last seen him perform some years before? Had I not filmed him in this very same role? After the rehearsals, we had talked endlessly about his Lear in the canteen and in the local bars. Carl had been so very proud of the new dimensions he had brought to the role, the uniqueness of his intonation as he attacked the wickedness of the world when declaring, Through tattered clothes, great vices do appear, robes and furred gowns hide all, plate sins with gold and the strong lance of justice hurtless breaks, arm it in rags, a pigmy's straw does pierce it, as he then contrasted this so poignantly with Lear's final quiet acceptance of his own condition, I am a very foolish fond old man…and to deal plainly, I fear I am not in my perfect mind.

My mind could not assimilate these two images, the Lear Carl had striven to create, and the Lear now slowly seeping from his very soul. Despite my best efforts, the old and the new Carl refused to be integrated. I, the master of the image, could no longer shape what I saw into a whole, could not contain this moment.

Was Carl still playing a role? Was he feigning a kind of madness in order to survive? Or had he donned his Hamlet mask in order to gain a heightened sense of what was happening? I couldn't decide. So I tried to see him as two different people, to convince myself that this person before me was not really the Carl I had known all those years ago. That he was only his look-alike. That I was mistaken. And without consciously realising it, I, too, was entering the madness of this place. I was allowing reality and illusion to become dangerously blurred.

Hours seemed to pass before I approached Carl. At first, he did not recognise me or my words, although I had carefully chosen my moment to interrupt him. We'd always had a kind of running gag when he was playing Lear. I used to tease him by telling him that he was born to play Mephistopheles and not Lear. That his Mephistopheles was far more convincing. As I reminded him of this again on that dreary January, I was not to know that he had been playing the role of Mephistopheles even in this place. And that his interpretation had gained him great accolade. Even here. Even now.

Carl, I can hardly see you! Give me that Mephistopheles line about darkness and light and the way darkness gave birth to light, I had playfully demanded as I forced myself into his world. His Lear dissolved away as he slowly turned his head to the direction from where my voice was coming. He didn't recognise me, that much I could sense from his quizzical expression. But he somehow knew that he should. He wanted to recognise my voice, he wanted to retrieve its origins from a far-removed past. And I assisted with another prompt, Hey, come on Carl, you know you play Mephistopheles better than Lear. You know Goethe wrote the greater tragedy.

Hitler's is the greatest, though! He quickly retorted, holding onto my eyes defiantly as he did so, until his face eventually quivered into a barely perceptible wry smile. His sense of irony had not abandoned him. I now knew that he had recognised me at last, and stealing one of his Mephistopheles' lines, I responded emphatically, Dust shall he swallow, aye, and love it. At which point his smile erupted into laughter bringing my disjointed world also back into some kind of order. We laughed together, united by the shared humour. Somehow, we both sensed intuitively that the tragedy of which we were a part, was a tragedy waiting to happen. Long gestating.

My Mephistopheles, I declared, as I patted him on the back, my Mephistopheles, I repeated. Hey, my Faust, Carl retaliated, suddenly remembering the name he'd always called me during our drinking sessions in Prague. The names we had once given one another shed little light on our personalities. Welcome to the best place on Earth! Bohemia – a Utopia! he then proclaimed, as he opened his arms to embrace the squalid barrack and to signal to me that his home was also my home. We fell into each other's arms. We, like long-lost friends, could unhesitatingly appreciate our affinity, our shared past.

During our Prague times, Carl had kept telling me that I should take up acting. It somehow irritated him that I preferred to view life through a lens. Carl wanted me on the stage, wanted me to experience the ebb and flow of the audience's feelings, wanted me to learn how to gauge and skilfully handle these, to make each performance a unique living moment, as he also learned how to develop his characters with each performance in an ongoing process of creation.

He'd admired my photographs of animals, long before he knew any of my stage work. He'd been impressed by my desire to penetrate the depths of nature, to seek out the essence of a being and capture it in an image. He once told me that it was my pictures that had opened his eyes a second time to nature. What poets could do with words, I had also achieved with my photographs, he'd said. But for some strange reason, he could not equate the unique glimpses of the wildlife which I'd captured, and which he'd so much admired, with the character insights he was conveying. When I showed him the stills of his characters, he turned away in obvious disapproval. It was as if he did not want them to become permanent. Petrified.

I was the opposite. I had wanted to capture and preserve time. The essence of a moment. The essence of a creation. I had wanted to freeze it and make it stand still. And then preserve it in shapes and forms, and with light and shade that I could render intriguing. With a shift of perspective, an unusual angle, I was able to capture a part of the whole and suddenly distort the whole moment. Displace it, enhance it, or question it. Carl could do this for his character with a gesture. But I could then choose to emphasise a different expression, a different feature, a different shade. It was a battle of effects, and of wills. The possibilities were endless. We both wanted to be master of the techniques, of the effect and of the creation. We were both exploring the infinity of space and time. The infinity of being. And in our own ways.

Did you notice the bank, he asked me, Did you notice the post-office, he persisted, alluding to the way our oppressors were trying to deceive the outside world into believing that this camp was really a normal town. I had not. They're all fake, can you believe it, he exclaimed, We're living in a make-believe world. We're all actors. Even, you my friend have now become an actor! Welcome to the trade! he quipped, and laughed heartily at this sudden insight. The tragedy is, I can no longer act, he added solemnly, I have been assigned the most important role of my life, and I can't play it. I've studied it from every angle, I've experimented with all aspects and still I can't find a way in. The script changes daily. And, do you know what, my Mephistopheles is as good as ever! Perhaps even better, yet, I've not developed the character in years. Not had the slightest inclination. It's all down to the audience…it's the audience that has developed, whilst I feel as though I've been turned inside out.

Maybe you need the cameraman, I assisted. Maybe I'm what you need. The one you always thought hindered your development and distorted your authenticity, I gently teased. Maybe, Carl replied, somewhat unresponsively. He seemed reluctant to engage with the intellectual arguments of the past. With intellectual words. They had understandably lost any sense of meaning in this continent within a continent. In this inhuman containment. It was the containment and the people and objects within it that spoke out, that reached him now.

Hang onto your hopes, my friend, he suddenly whispered from nowhere, with great tenderness, They're what you'll need right now. Here. And if you can't, build them again. For me, it's perhaps too late. I've had sixty-eight good years and two less good ones. But you have many yet to live, many beyond this Hell. Hang onto them, that's the only worthwhile advice I can give you right now. And then, with a good portion of pathos in his voice, he continued, The past is best forgotten. Bury it. Revive it when you have a future. When you know you have a future.

Carl's sense of the dramatic had also not abandoned him, I remember thinking on that late afternoon in January. I had arrogantly and instantly dismissed his words of warnings. I had treated them as an extension of Carl's reality, and had not made the connection to this place to which I was still a stranger. A non-initiate. I had not taken them seriously. I was the fool.

And now, my friend, let's find you a bed. Let's find you a dwelling in this great castle, Carl wryly proclaimed, whilst gesturing to be led.

~ ~ ~

Funnily enough it was that first exchange which had created a new kind of complicity between us. The beginnings of a different kind of play-acting had emerged, but one for which a camera lens, or at least an imagined one, could have a place. It was during that surreal encounter in the barracks that I realised that my cameraman techniques may perhaps help us both survive this hell-hole together.

The game went like this, whenever we were feeling low and crushed by the circumstances, one of us would suddenly say, Hey you, show me your wild streak, show me the animal in you, your untamed side! And the trick was to adopt a defiant pose. A pose for the pretend camera. And after the pretend shot had been taken, the other had to guess the animal that had been imitated. With hindsight this now seemed rather banal and silly, but at the time it helped to lift us out of an ever-threatening and ever-increasing sense of depression.

We had both become cameramen, just as we'd both become actors. The camera, even the pretend one, provided us with the necessary distance, the life-saving distance. I could train Carl to see the world around him with the eye of a camera lens. That was my goal. And with the animal antics, we'd try and remind ourselves of our wild streaks. Of our humanity. Our humanity was the wild streak, that's what I kept telling Carl. The streak that told us that we could be whoever or whatever we wanted to be. It was the part of us that was the only truth. It was also the part that would not acquiesce under any condition. To any brutality.

Our humanity was the tiger's eye, it was our essence, it was our spirit. And it was what I had learnt all those years ago from the animals I'd photographed on the Steppes. In the wilderness. But also from the ones I'd photographed in the zoo. During my hours of circling the cages, of unobtrusively observing their every gesture and expression, I'd become aware of the subtle defiance of their nature, of the quiet stubbornness of individual animals even when caged, even when humiliated and removed from their natural environment. It was that that I'd wanted to capture all those years ago. Their essence, which was also our essence.

During the first few weeks of our togetherness, I'd also managed to convince Carl of this. I'd managed to assist him in a new role. A role focused on playfulness, but no less serious. A role for which Carl was born. It was the role of the humorist. A role which he'd played so convincingly as Mephistopheles. Mephistopheles, the great humorist, yet Carl had failed to appreciate his own talent, his own unique interpretation of the role. He'd so wanted to excel with his Lear, it was with Lear he'd wanted to become one, not with Mephistopheles. That was the tragedy of his acting career. His Mephistopheles had always outshone his Lear.

Carl was from the German-speaking part of Czechoslovakia, I was from the Czech-speaking part. We were now united by our race, before it had been the theatre. And the irony was, we were both atheists, or rather humanists, and knew or cared very little about our shared religious roots. We had considered ourselves to be human beings, cosmopolitan in outlook and ways. Yet, at this point in time, and in this part of Europe, it was our so-called inherited blood which was now significant. It was this that singled us out for special confinement, for punishment. This place was only ever intended as a staging post, as I would later discover. We were destined for a greater Hell. For Hell Unlimited. Carl already knew that. He'd already been here too long.

It was I, however, who would be the one better equipped for coping with the increasing brutalities. It was I who had watched through my lens as the lion tore apart its victim. It was I who had carefully studied the killing, waiting patiently for the perfect image. Animals killed to eat. They did not persecute their victims. I knew the distinction. But perhaps as an avid voyeur to these acts of killing, I too had compromised my humanity.

~ ~ ~

No matter how many times I've died on stage – and I've had many great memorable deaths – do you know what, my friend, this hasn't prepared me for the true depths of death and dying, Carl began to open up, as he shuffled along with me down one of the mud-strewn streets now streaked with the white of freshly fallen snow. Just as the great roles I've played had not prepared me for life. They'd shielded me from it. Before this place I'd died all the noble deaths. Convincingly. Authentically. If the applause is a measurement of success. Yet, it's only now, only here, that I realise that I'd merely scratched the surface. At the time, though, I'd deceived myself into thinking that I was at one with my part, that I knew the depths…that life and death flowed through my body, that my senses were alive, that I was the beholder of the ancient magic powers of acting. My friend, it is here in this place that I feel Faust…a dark poetic Faust, a Faust intoxicated by his senses. Not the pleasurable kind. But nevertheless ones which make your head spin. They are real. I feel them all the time.

How could I ever have imagined that it was enough to read and interpret the feelings written about in the great works? That I then would know. Know what the character was feeling. Feel that I was giving him life. Real life. Ah! Romantic nonsense, the lot of it! My friend, it is here that I have learnt to read the signs. The dark feelings. The dark motives. How can I act now, when I can no longer deny the unimaginable horrors around me? They're tearing at the threads of my sanity.

Carl struggled to make contact with the space in which he now found himself, within this camp disguised as a town. Although in many ways it was still a set he was working on. Not artificial, not in the sense of the theatre…it was for real, and the setting in which he was forced to act was being changed daily. It was treacherously slippery. There was no segregation between stage and auditorium for guidance. It was hard to know or predict when one would be thrust on stage, and when one would be part of the audience. Here, it was the drama of the place presenting the actor, it was not the actor presenting the drama, and as such, the visual and oral outbursts were unpredictable. And the physical outbursts knew no bounds. This is why Carl was still struggling to make contact with the place. He was still adopting his painfully and patiently learnt methods, he was thinking with his whole body, reacting with all of it.

My training had been different. I had learnt how to be patient, how to watch the wilderness change before my lens, how to detach myself from the surroundings. I had learnt how to read the unpredictability, to record the images before me and then freeze them with a click of the button. I had learnt how to be in the service of creatures. For as long as was necessary. For the perfect image. And here I found another kind of wilderness-cum-zoo. It was as if the designers were trying to bring the whole of nature into a kind of theatre of their own making. A total theatre. No longer dependent, however, upon a juxtaposition of imagery, but rather a juxtaposition of realities. Brutal realities.

And it's strange to realise with hindsight that I'd felt and thought all this on that first afternoon with Carl. An impression of a Theatre of

Cruelty. Of a Theatre of Cruelty in life. Where life would lose everything, and the mind would gain everything. The sadistic mind. The sadistic mind in pursuit of blood, torture and murder.

As Carl consented to be led, I saw for the first time the open sores on his hands and face. The threadbare hat which he'd retrieved from the floor, and which now perched precariously on his head, did little to hide his swollen eye crusting up with pus. The inside of his lips were also unevenly puffed up with small congealed black clusters. His fine set of teeth, always meticulously well cleaned and manicured, now hung crookedly and limply in his mouth. They were thickly coated with tartar and caked with bits of rotting bread and potato. Many were missing.

~ ~ ~

There was quite a commotion in the street nearby as we turned a corner. People were gathering for the last warm sustenance of the day in front of the kitchens. Some kind of murky-coloured liquid was being hurriedly ladled out. Clutching tin mugs, misshapen bowls and any old receptacle, men, women, and children of all ages were queuing eagerly next to the large containers. Instinctively, and like one of Pavlov's dogs, Carl reached into the inside of his coat and pulled out a battered and heavily stained mug, Hey, my friend, and remember, this is your most valuable possession from now on, he suddenly bellowed as he held his mug up to my nose, Guard it with your life, he warned.

Carl's thick woollen coat with its light tweed and herringbone weave was torn and tattered. Bigger patches of cloth had been sewn onto smaller ones, and even these were now fraying at the edges. The coat was drawn together by a rusty old belt, and, as Carl snatched out his mug, a few crumpled photographs fell to the floor. There was no time for me to bend down and pick them up for him. Carl had rushed to retrieve and repossess these faded images as quickly as possible.

I guessed that the elderly couple dressed in rather old-fashioned looking, yet somewhat exotic clothes must have been his parents. Judging by the brownish hue, it was a photograph which had been taken many years earlier. Carl also had a few photographs of himself in his younger days and in them he was dressed in various costumes. His Lear was among them, his Mephistopheles was not.

On catching sight of his Lear again he began to reminisce. And immediately he slipped back into role, back into his Lear, the one that I remembered so clearly from the past, the one that bore little resemblance to the real figure of Lear which I had espied on first entering the barrack.

Instead of his hat perched on his head, I imagined him crowned with wild flowers, as he began to utter some lines of mad King Lear.

Look, look a mouse: peace, peace, this piece of toasted cheese will do't. And as Carl bent down to retrieve a pretend bit of cheese to lure the pretend mouse, people in the queue turned their heads and began to listen to him as he continued with a defiant and dramatic gesture, There's my gauntlet, I'll prove it on a giant. At which point many of his onlookers burst into laughter.

Knowing that he now had a captive audience, he began to excel once more in his role, They flattered me like a dog, he declaimed, And told me I had the white hairs in my beard ere the black ones were there. To say 'ay' and 'no' to everything that I said 'ay' and 'no' to was no good divinity. When the rain came to wet me once and the wind to make me chatter, when the thunder would not peace at my bidding, there I found 'em, there I smelt 'em out. Carl screwed up his face to make it as ugly as possible before resuming in a mock self-pitying tone, which was also intended to make fun of the Lear he was portraying, Go to, they are not men o'their words, they told me I was everything, 'tis a lie, I am not ague-proof.

If Carl could still make fun of his and our plight, if he could still manage to capture the absurdity of the situation, yet without directly referring to it, then all was not lost, I thought. And he'd certainly managed to bring a smile to the faces of those around him. Even here, even now. And, now I too began to join in with the light relief, The trick of that voice I do well remember, is't not the King? I inquired, as I pressed my face closely against his.

Ay, every inch a King in this castle, he boasted as he thrust forward his chest, extended his neck and pushed me away from him before continuing in a grandiose and commanding voice, When I do stare, see how the subject quakes, and with this he fixed his eyes on a young boy of about eleven or twelve who was standing a few yards in front of us. It was evident from the boy's puzzled look that he was not sure whether to show respect to this mad King, or to burst out laughing. His indecisiveness manifested itself in a blush.

Then Carl quickly turned his attention to a young man in the queue who had been closely following Carl's antics, I pardon that man's life, what was thy cause? Adultery? Thou shalt not die – die for adultery? No! The young man was a friend of Carl's. They'd come to this place on the same transport. Carl knew he could play with him mercilessly and that the man would understand his intention, The wren goes to't and the small gilded fly does lecher in my sight. Let copulation thrive, Carl declared, and he too joined in with the laughter that now erupted all around him and he swung his mug to and fro in time to the hysterical outbursts.

After months of observing his Lear, I had also internalised the lines of the play, many poignant ones came flooding back to me. I, like the motley audience now gathered around Carl, revelled in the rich poetic utterances, in the delicacies and depth of his portrayal of human character. In an instant, the atmosphere seemed to have changed. Even the murky-coloured salty liquid seemed quite palatable. That, too, was an illusion.

Lena, come and join us, Carl suddenly called out to a slenderly built woman huddled over her bowl and clutching at a book half-hidden from view. Let me introduce you to my long-lost friend, to my drinking partner. Lena had been following Carl's mischief from afar. She'd also chuckled as she'd watched him move amongst the queue as mad King Lear.

My friend, meet the finest Greta I've ever known! A Greta to end all Gretas, he quipped, and winked knowingly at her. Thirty times she's died because of me, he declared, Thirty times, and each time more poignant than the last. And tonight, she'll die again, my friend. And, if you have anything we can use as a bribe, you, too, can be a witness.

The grotesqueness of Carl's comments seemed to escape him. How could Goethe's Faust be performed in this place, I wondered. For Carl and Lena, it already seemed quite natural to be talking about the tragedy. To be acting it here. Now. But for me, a newcomer to life in a camp, and until a few days ago a fugitive in hiding, it all seemed so bizarre. My last two years had been spent painstakingly avoiding strangers, moving about in friends' apartments only after nightfall, taking every precaution possible to erase the tiniest trace of my existence. And now? And now I could see a performance of Faust. By inmates. Under the noses of the guards. Here?

But, my friend, we have to find you a ticket, that's not going to be easy. Our Faust was sold out months ago, it's the talk of the town, you see. And with this, Carl burst into laughter once more. As he caught sight of the completely bewildered look on my face, Carl sensed how ridiculous this must all seem to an outsider. He had read my thoughts. His gaze penetrated my eyes, he held me in a transfixed state, inhaled deeply, sighed a long sigh and then nudged his mug into the air again, as if to offer a toast to our friendship.

And now, to work, my friend. Lena will organise the ticket, won't you, Lena? Before waiting for her response, Carl grabbed hold of the shoulder of my coat, To work, he proclaimed once more, To work which has a meaning greater than all this. And with that, Carl stood up from the bench on which he'd perched himself, offered me his arm and guided me towards an attic room at the top of one of the barracks. The attic room would be the venue not only for the evening's performance of Faust, but also the space in which the youngsters would soon be gathering for their acting classes. Their secret acting classes.

You know what you were saying about Goethe's Faust being better than Shakespeare's Lear, well you're quite wrong, declared Carl, taking up the conversation again as we entered the attic room, I'm not so sure that I'd call Faust a tragedy, not in the real sense. Lear is the really tragic figure, the one who loses everything and gains nothing.

Madness, Carl, madness, that's what Lear gains, I protested instinctively, not realising that Carl was deliberately provoking me into a response, Madness and, with it, insight and love for his youngest and truest daughter Cordelia.

Madness, ah yes, madness, you're right, agreed Carl, Lear's madness is not a burden, it's a revelation, and it's in his madness that we see, see what he suddenly sees – his own humanity, his own frail humanity. But it's all too late. Far too late. That's the tragedy. His intentions are essentially good, he wanted to be loved and for that love to be publicly declared. Faust, my friend, is altogether different, Faust is about life, it embraces all human life, life and activity, and that's what keeps me sane. Activity. Now. Here, even here, my friend. I'm not so sure that King Lear could be read or performed here, but Faust can be, why, you'll see that for yourself, you'll hear the applause, you'll see the reactions. My friend, over thirty times we've performed Faust here. Hamlet, Othello, these are performed here too, performed for an audience, but not King Lear. Yet, I feel Lear in every waking moment, and even in my sleep. In my private moments, when I think I'm alone, I enact the tragedy, it's cathartic, you see. My friend, it's my own private catharsis. I lose myself in Lear's anger, grief and loss. And so I discharge my own pent-up emotions. That's what I was doing, my friend, when you found me. That's what I try to do daily.

Does any here know me? Carl dramatically declared as he scanned the empty attic room as if it were the Great Hall at Goneril's castle. Goneril, the daughter who has just inherited from him and simultaneously betrayed him. Why, this is not Lear, does Lear walk thus, speak thus, where are his eyes? Either his notion weakens, or his discernings are lethargied – ha! sleeping or waking? Sure 'tis not so. Who is it that can tell me who I am?

Lear's shadow, I interjected very softly, then, in a more playful voice, And very much my Carl, my Mephistopheles! I mischievously declared.

O Lear, Lear, Lear! cried Carl as he struck his head, unswayed by my jocularity, Beat at this gate that let thy folly in and thy dear judgement out. Go, go, my people.

Did Carl also want me to leave? It was difficult to tell, so absorbed was he now in Lear, Hear, Nature, hear, dear goddess, hear, suspend thy purpose if thou didst intend to make this creature fruitful. Into her womb convey sterility, and from her derogate body never spring a babe to honour her.

No, stop, my friend, don't leave, Carl suddenly called across to me in an altogether different tone of voice, as if only now remembering my presence, as I attempted to slip out of the building, I speak these words and I have in mind Germany. This is my catharsis, Germany is the daughter that has betrayed me. When I utter this speech, I utter revenge. It gives me the will power and strength of mind to continue, to continue here. I get rid of any bitterness and anger in private, and am free for my youngsters, free to guide them towards a different life and hopefully to new lives.

Carl continued his rant, moving slowly round the attic room as he did so and lifting his eyes now and again towards the rafters, Life and death, I am ashamed that thou hast power to shake my manhood thus, that these hot tears which break from me perforce, should make thee worth them, blasts and fogs upon thee! Carl shook his fist in the air as he worked himself up into an uncontrollable rage.

His vexatious tones still hung in the air as he fell to his knees, covered his face, and then turned to me, You know, Austria also betrayed me. I sought refuge in Austria, too, and she also turned her back on me. O let me not be mad, not mad, sweet heaven! Carl declared, as he lifted his eyes upwards once more to the bare roof rafters, Keep me in temper, I would not be mad.

Let go thy hold when a great wheel runs down a hill, I rejoined, taking on the role of Lear's fool once more, Lest it break thy neck with following it, but the great one that goes upward, let him draw thee after. Then completely carried away by the moment, I leaped to my feet and began to hop around Carl chanting, That sir which serves and seeks for gain, and follows but for form, will pack when it begins to rain and leave thee in a storm, but I will tarry, the fool will stay, and let the wise man fly, the knave turns fool that runs away, the fool no knave perdy.

Carl watched a while as I pranced around him. He then let out a long hearty laugh, enjoying the fun of the moment, You see, my friend, Faust keeps me active here, keeps me performing, but it's Lear that is in my soul, it's Lear that I keep feeling, it is Lear to whom I instinctively turn. Isn't it strange, it is as if it is Lear's own madness that is saving me from my own. And tonight, my friend, yes, tonight, you will have your Mephistopheles, And so onwards over graves! At which point, Carl laughed once more. Only this time it was the scornful laugh of Mephistopheles. Then, in an altogether intimate tone, he turned to me and confided, You know, my friend, it is only here that I begin to understand myself. Isn't that tragic? Carl held my gaze with his and searched expectantly into my eyes, All that acting on the best stages in Europe, in America, and it didn't help me to get closer to who I am. All those brief affairs and wonderful liaisons. All that drinking in bars with you and talking until the early hours of the morning. Then as if he sensed that he might hurt my feelings, he drew my shoulder towards his and squeezed it tightly, But, my friend, we had our good times, our fun times, and they too seem all the more poignant now.

But that's not what Carl really wanted to tell me, it was as if he'd been fleeing from himself, or avoiding confronting and understanding himself, that's what he was really telling me. He'd been happy to be who the audience and devotees deemed him to be. Who I deemed him to be. Only now, only here, he sensed the shallowness of that life. The wastefulness. The wasted moments. This was the Lear I found before me, and I now knew that my first impression had been quite wrong. It was here that Carl not only connected with himself but also with the youngsters. And it was especially the youngsters who kept him active. Through working with them he achieved his highest aim, a real role in life. It was as if this were the task he'd been born to fulfil and the one which would mark the climax of his life. Faust's departing words on Earth, I later reflected, could have been Carl's, Foretasting such high happiness to come, I savour now my striving's crown and sum.

Strange though it may seem to non-initiates of this place, some of the inmates did experience moments of oneness, in spite of the brutal conditions that were evident everywhere. I remember that clearly now. There really were times when inmates could become so absorbed in an activity that they could forget who they were and where they were. If only briefly. They could find some kind of purpose beyond their own existence. Or at least, some could. I observed this most with Carl. Carl dedicated his non-working time to training the youngsters in the art of acting. But more importantly, he was facilitating an education for life.

~ ~ ~

The first youngsters began to assemble in the attic room soon after we had arrived. Despite their dishevelled appearance, their eyes widened when they caught sight of Carl pacing up and down the room, lost once more in thought and mumbling words under his breath, then stopping and gesticulating to the walls. There were about twenty or so eleven to fifteen year olds this evening.

Carl wanted the session to focus on Hamlet, and had managed to procure two battered copies, around which groups of youngsters soon huddled. It was to be the first of a series of sessions on the play. He didn't want to tell them anything about the way Hamlet had been perceived over the years, especially in Germany. He wanted the youngsters to discover their own meaning about Hamlet, the Danish prince, and Hamlet the play. He also didn't want to tell them how Shakespeare had become a German Shakespeare for many – so much had the Germans identified with the poet and his work. And hadn't it been Goethe who had first alluded to the German Hamlet?

Why, let the stricken deer go weep, the hart ungallèd play, for some must watch, while some must sleep, so runs the world away, began a young boy of about fourteen, as he sat cross-legged on the bare floorboards, whilst another boy held the candle stub close to the text. Would not this, sir, and a forest of feathers, if the rest of my fortunes turn Turk with me, with two Provencal roses on my razed shoes, get me a fellowship in a cry of players, sir? Half a share, declared a young girl, taking on the part of Horatio. A whole one, I, continued the young boy as Hamlet, For thou dost know, O Damon dear, this realm dismantled was of Jove himself, and now reigns here a very, very – patchcock.

Carl wanted to let them play with the text and encouraged them to read it in different voices and moods, until they had settled upon the right one for them. This caused great laughter, and the youngsters appeared to delight in the language, the colourfulness and the strangeness of it. They sensed the general meaning and didn't seem to be too bothered about the details or the specifics. Instead, they had great fun pretending to be part of a royal household, part of a bygone era, and they adopted all kinds of strange and affected voices. Another favourite source of playfulness was for the youngsters to try and read the text to the rhythm that others rapped out on the wooden floorboards. Some of the youngsters would deliberately begin to rap ever more quickly so as to cause the readers to trip up on the words as they struggled to keep pace.

Carl guided the youngsters into finding something in the text which appealed to them and encouraged them to focus on that and to form a voice, an intonation or a mood around it. Make a note of the word on your scraps of paper, he'd say, Draw something in response to it, he'd advise. Anything. It doesn't matter. What is important is that it is your own unique response, your own internalisation.

At one point during the session, Carl retrieved a book with photographs from under the floorboards of the attic. The book was full of scenes from Shakespeare's plays performed on the German stages in the twenties and thirties and this book was eagerly seized upon by the youngsters. They stared intently at the black and white photos of the heroes and heroines, but also of the villains. They scrutinised each and every contour of the faces and playfully imitated the different postures.

The youngsters were especially eager to learn this week, Carl later told me. One of the transports heading East had taken over a thousand inmates with it a couple of days before I had arrived. The youngsters knew that they may never see some of their relatives again. Although the adults seldom spoke directly about the deportations and their fears, the youngsters nevertheless seemed to know and sense what it was all about.

Carl's mission was to set the children free through the creative powers of acting, to get them to fall in love with the art-form, to get them to forget the sadness and misery. But he also wanted to let their creativity unfold in a free and natural way.

These are the beginnings of your own special journey, Carl told the youngsters, A journey which needs to take you as artists to the depths of your soul, Carl continued, The artist must develop and tend upon it, so that his or her art has something to clothe and does not remain a glove without a hand, he emphasized, referring to Kandinsky's view of the spiritual in art. Carl had become acquainted with Kandinsky in the twenties and they'd immediately bonded.

In understanding a character in a play, Carl stressed, The artist must first search the character's soul, every inch of it, and then let his or her own soul speak with the character's until they became as one. That it was only through this internal dialogue, Carl confided, that his own Lear or Mephistopheles could be born and could be believed on stage. That it was up to each artist to find a path leading inward to the spirit, and that even Goethe's Mephistopheles had such a path, Carl said.

My own personal way into a character is through colour and tone of voice, I remember him telling the youngsters that evening. I often experiment with thousands upon thousands of shades of colour and tonal aspects, and let them vibrate and resound within me until I settle upon the aura of the character. But once I've discovered the aura and primeval power which is unique to the character, each word that I utter comes from this foundation. From this infusion. And he gesticulated to his lower abdomen. I then work in unison with my own and with my character's spirit, he said, They are embodied as one. I, however, was fascinated by the primeval power in all creation, by the forces which create the world and especially by nature as it manifests itself to us. Strange though it may seem, my fascination only increased in this place… Here, too, I was eager to see what held this world together, what forces were at the bottom of it all.

Carl could still vie with nature with his creative powers, I thought, as I listened intently to what he was telling the youngsters. As I watched their faces, I could see that they had become mesmerised by what he was saying, that they were forgetting the wretchedness of their surroundings and situation, and were allowing themselves to be lifted to a higher plane of experience. However, it was in their own experimentation with a character of their choice, that they could truly abandon their conscious selves.

Carl always began his sessions with breathing and rhythmic exercises. He used his acting experience to evoke a sense of spiritual transcendence in the youngsters he taught, and by so doing, encouraged them to find and experience their own sense of time and space, and to inhabit their own parallel world. Most importantly, he was creating a few magical moments that were far removed from the immediate horrors.

They were moments that transformed their everyday world and propelled the youngsters into realms of the infinite and into the depths of total absorption of another self. That, too, fascinated me.

But perhaps most of all I appreciated our discussions on Goethe and Shakespeare. Crazy though it may now sound, it was these talks which also kept us going, which kept our minds alive and active, and free from the prison in which we found ourselves for most of the waking day. And yet, they still did not protect me from myself…

Hey, come on, Carl, I'd provocatively protested after the youngsters had left and before the audience for that evening's performance of Faust had arrived, Should you really be teaching Shakespeare here? Have you forgotten his Merchant of Venice? Hasn't Shakespeare done a great disservice to Jews by creating Shylock, a Jew intent on gaining his pound of flesh at all costs?

But it's not Shakespeare's Shylock, he'd insisted, Shylock is the sum of all our Shylocks down the ages, look at how the other characters in the play talk about him, they hate him, even his daughter seems to despise him. Shylock is to be pitied, people and circumstances have made him into what he is. At which point Carl took on the role of Shylock and thrust the role of Antonio, the Merchant of Venice, upon me, saying, Signior Antonio, many a time and oft in the Rialto you have rated me about my moneys and my usances, still have I borne it with a patient shrug for sufferance is the badge of all our tribe. You call me misbeliever, cut throat, dog and spit upon my Jewish gaberdine and all for use of that which is mine own.

Okay, Carl, okay. Shakespeare showed both Christians and Jews at one another's throat, why do you think I'm an atheist, I remembered saying.

But not just that, my friend, Carl resumed in his own voice, He also shows us what happens when emotions and money clash. We see how Shylock's insistence on the letter of a contract poisons his soul. He destroys himself. His sterility is borne out of the cold world of commerce in Venice, the play is not really about Christians and Jews, this here, this now, is not really about Christians and Jews, this is about money, about power and money, and the hatred and fear which both breed. Antonio and Shylock are as one, financial rivals, Shakespeare shows us this, they are united in their hate for one another and their love of money. Perhaps Antonio would have also demanded his pound of flesh, if the shoe had been on the other foot, who knows?

Carl let these last words hang in the air, in the dank air of the draughty and foul-smelling attic, before continuing, The characters around Shylock are anti-Semitic, Shylock is being persecuted from all sides, he lives in a pernicious society, in a society in which moral values have become tainted. Money, greed and commercial contracts have corrupted the society. We know this, my friend, we know. And my friend, look about you here, see how this place also corrupts and demonises our souls through fear, hunger and the rough necessities of survival. It has been designed that way. And we deal with it in different ways, and your way will be different to mine. Can you look me in the eye and tell me honestly that you, too, will not demand your pound of flesh when you leave this place? Will you really be able to turn your back on all this, on everything that you have seen, on everything that you have been a part of? Have you not already made a contract with yourself? A pact. Not just with yourself?

Carl knew me well. Too well. He sensed the workings of my mind. He sensed how I would be feeling inside, even as I tried to conceal and suppress my emotions. He was more in touch with me than I was with myself. I now know. Unlike Carl, I was not working on my emotions and my attitude towards some higher ideal. For the most part I was suppressing them, blocking them out and directing my energies towards observing, and towards mentally recording my environment.

Look at the contracts the oppressed have had to sign just in the last few years, Carl continued, Look at the way they've had to sign over houses and possessions in order to leave the country, in order to start another life, in order to survive. And look at the inmates here, look at the old and sick who bought their so-called haven here, look at the contracts they signed and the way they have been mercilessly deceived.

You're right Carl, maybe it is greed that lies at the heart of all this. Greed and utter corruption, I conferred, Schopenhauer was right, the world is Hell, and men are on the one hand the tormented souls and on the other the devils in it. Mephistopheles and Faust conjoined, that sums it all up. Goethe got it right.

I knew this last remark would be irresistible for Carl, that he would evoke his Shakespeare. The web of our life is of a mingled yarn, good and ill together, countered Carl in a wistful voice, then continuing in an altogether different timbre and with a sense of urgency, Greed, power, hatred and corruption are the forces against which man has battled since time immemorial, and will always do so, even after this. But we must teach the youngsters about a world of different values, continued Carl defiantly, Of different forces that we can all help to shape. In the future. But we can sow the seeds now, we can live it in our minds now, we can talk about it now, my friend, we must do what we can to create this different world, Carl urged, Otherwise all this here, all this now, will be our future, and the Hell will be never-ending.

But Carl didn't allow our discussion to end on this ominous note. After a short pause, he turned to me, looked me directly and challengingly in the eye, before declaring in a matter-of-fact yet confident way, Mephistopheles will not win, I simply won't allow it. And then Carl's facial muscles, held so tautly for this last comment, relaxed into a broad smile which rippled out from the centre of his face before erupting into a laugh which almost swallowed his eyes completely – eyes which still shone with defiance through the laughter.

~ ~ ~

How Lena had managed to get hold of a ticket for me on my first evening in this place, I'll never know. She didn't say. And it somehow hadn't seemed that important to ask. I had entered into the reality of this place. Effortlessly. Into Faust. A strange Faust, that much I do remember thinking that evening. A heightened Faust. Although the words were not enacted, but rather read out loud, they nevertheless took on a life of their own. A new life. It was as if the tragedy were being told for the very first time. As if the whole history of the

Faustian tragedy and of Faust's pact with the devil were previously unknown.

The words burst into being, they danced, they flirted, they sang, they whispered, they cried, they cursed, they screamed. They also fell silent. It was the silences that I remember more than the words. The silence between words, between acts, between roles. The silence between life and death. The kind of silence that conjures up memories.

And then there was Gretchen. I didn't see Lena. I saw only Gretchen before me. This place must have already encroached upon my senses for me to feel the sentiments of the play so intensely. I saw only Gretchen's love and tenderness. Although Lena didn't leave her chair as she read the lines, Gretchen moved before me. But, it wasn't Gretchen either, I later realised. It was my own first real love that suddenly reared its head from nowhere, which suddenly gripped every muscle in my body and kept me in a heightened state of spasmodic desire. I'd not known such a complete hold on my emotions for a long time.

O tremble not! declared Faust, But let this look, let this warm clasp of hands declare thee what is unspeakable! To yield one wholly, and to feel a rapture in yielding, that must be eternal! Eternal! For the end would be despair. No, no — no ending! No ending! As the reading was nearing the final act, and at the point when Faust learns from Mephistopheles that Gretchen is in the dungeon and awaiting her execution for the killing of her newly born baby, I let my eyes roam once more around the attic room and rest upon the motley collection of faces peering out of the darkness. Their gaunt faces no longer expressed sadness and exhaustion, as they had on first arriving in the attic room. They had come to life. I, too, had come to life.

The attentiveness was astonishing, quite bewildering. Faust, on learning of Gretchen's fate and impending execution, and suddenly feeling guilt at his devilish seduction of her with the help of Mephistopheles, turned to Carl playing Mephistopheles, and in a rage declared, Dog! Abominable monster! And then, turning his eyes upwards, Faust cried deploringly, Transform him, thou Infinite Spirit, transform the reptile again into his dog-shape, in which it pleased him often at night to scamper on before me, to roll himself at the feet of the unsuspecting wanderer, and hang upon his shoulders when he fell! Then he paused slightly, before pleading even more desperately, with his hands now tightly clasped together and with revenge in his eye, Transform him again into his favourite likeness, that he may crawl upon his belly in the dust before me, that I may trample him, the outlawed, under my foot! And then in a quieter voice, the actor playing Faust continued,

Not the first! o woe! woe which no human soul can grasp, that more than one being should sink into the depths of this misery, that the first, in its writhing death-agony under the eyes of the Eternal Forgiver, did not expiate the guilt of all the others! And then turning once more to Mephistopheles whose face he now perused with a mixture of both hatred and necessity, before continuing, The misery of this single one pierces to the very marrow of my life, and thou art calmly grinning at the fate of thousands!

Carl as Mephistopheles, tauntingly, and now with a snarl on his face, Why did you enter into fellowship with us, if you cannot carry it out? Want to fly, and are not secure against dizziness? Did we thrust ourselves upon you, or you yourself upon us? Who was it that plunged her into ruin? I, or you? And on hearing Faust's plea to be taken to Gretchen and to free her, Mephistopheles continued, remembering Faust's own role in Gretchen's brother's death, And the danger to which you will expose yourself? Know that the guilt of blood, from your hand, still lies upon the town! Avenging spirits hover over the spot where the victim fell, and lie in wait for the returning murderer.

That, too, from you? cried Faust in despair, Murder and death of a world upon you, monster! Take me there, I say, and liberate her!

The power of the words was electrifying. Carl was magnificent in his display of demonic tones and gestures. The whole room soon filled with the urgency of the situation, with the fateful devilishness, and with Faust's desperate act to save Gretchen. The audience knew the outcome. They knew that Gretchen would not, could not be saved. Not in this version. They knew, and yet they listened to the story as if they had never heard it before. As if the story went beyond the Faust legend and extended into the present. They knew that Gretchen would decline to be saved when Faust comes for her. For it was not Faust alone who could save her. They knew that she knew that it was really Mephistopheles who would be freeing her from her earthly prison, and it was him, the satanic figure, she refused, not Faust. It was Mephistopheles that had the power over their fate, and she declined to enter into his pact. She was stronger than Faust.

Just will it! Open stands the door, pleaded Faust to Gretchen on finding her in the dungeon, I dare not go, rejoined Gretchen, There's no hope any more. Why should I fly? They'll still my steps waylay! It is so wretched, forced to beg my living! And a bad conscience sharper misery giving! It is so wretched, to be strange, forsaken. And I'd still be followed and taken! I'll stay with you, declared Faust, grabbing hold of Gretchen's clasped hands,

Be quick! was her sharp response, Save your perishing child! she suddenly implored, remembering in her confused state the child she'd drowned, Be quick, follow the ridge up by the brook, over the bridge, into the wood, to the left, where the plank is placed in the pool! Seize it in haste! 'Tis trying to rise, 'Tis struggling still! Save it! Save it! Faust heard but could not see, and countered in desperation, Recall your wandering will! One step, and you are free at last! Here words and prayers are nothing worth, I'll venture, then, to bear you forth.

Gretchen, now completely at one with her fate, and without hesitation decried, No, Let me go! I'll suffer no force! Grasp me not so murderously! I've done, else, all things for the love of you. To which Faust, on seeing the morn of execution approach, helplessly responded, The day dawns! Dearest! Dearest!

The death-bell tolls, the wand is broken. I am seized, and bound, and delivered, shoved to the block, they give the sign! continued Gretchen quietly, yet with a great sense of inner strength and resolve, Now over each neck has quivered the blade that is quivering over mine. Dumb lies the world like the grave!

The reading lasted for nearly two hours, but there was no hint of salvation, not in this version of the text, not in Goethe's early draft.

And just like at any theatre performance or play-reading the performers were applauded and celebrated at the end. About one hundred inmates had crammed into the small space, and they now broke out into cheering. It was a genuine kind of appreciation, it was not forced or affected.

It wasn't the word, it was the action that counted, one of the members of the audience had written in her notebook that night, These battles of ideas must continue to be fought, come what may! She had found her Goethe again, here, in this place, and she had felt incredibly uplifted by the evening.

My next encounter with Lena was a few days later. I caught sight of her in one of the attic rooms above the children's barracks. She was crouching on the floor and small children were gathered round her. They were acting out a fairytale. The children were pretending to be sea creatures swimming around a rock. The rock was Lena. Lena was telling them that the rock held many wonderful powers and secrets and that if they sang to the rock in a certain way, then the rock would yield something very special.

When I peered through the open doorway, all I could hear were half lines from unfamiliar nursery rhymes which the children were testing out on the pretend rock. They were having great fun laughing at each other's efforts and climbing on top of Lena as they sang what they could remember of tunes they'd been inventing together.

Suddenly Lena said something. 'Yippee'! 'yippee'! screamed the children who had crowded in on her. From the inside of her jacket, Lena had just pulled out pieces of dumpling-like substance which she carefully deposited into the sea of outstretched waving palms. The children sank to the floor with eyes transfixed on their little treasure. Some gazed at it for a further few moments, others eagerly popped it into their shrunken mouths. The game thus came to a natural end and I stood observing the scene, unnoticed. The children played with the piece of dumpling and allowed it to linger on their tongues. Soon a dark cream-like substance crept out of the corners of their mouths as they bit into the centre. I suspected that many had not had such food for quite some time. Their eyes, now partly closed, became glazed over by the sensation and a soothing silence descended upon the room. Lena sat quietly amongst the children, happy just to watch them eat. Their pleasure was also hers.

Some time passed before she noticed me. I didn't thank you properly for the ticket the other night, I called from the doorway, as the children slowly drifted out of the room in small groups and made their way back down to their barracks, giggling away to each other, I hadn't realised how very difficult it must have been for you to get hold of it at such short notice.

Well, it must have been strange for you, Lena immediately replied, smiling at me as she did so, though still remaining seated on the wooden floor, I can't think it was easy for you experiencing Faust on your first night here. She was about to rise to her feet but then spotted an insect crawling up her leg which she swiftly disposed of. She briskly straightened her threadbare jacket and skirt as she eased herself up from the floor and quickly adjusted the cotton headscarf knotted round her head before approaching me.

It certainly wasn't what I was expecting on my first night. I'd heard rumours about this place, but I hadn't heard about these kind of activities. Did you act before coming here?

Lena told me that she hadn't. In fact, much of the theatre she'd experienced before coming here had been political, and had had very little to do with the classics. That was perhaps why she was enjoying Faust so much, she said, it was pure distraction for her. Lena went on to tell me that she had been born in Poland but had spent much of her time travelling before the war, and was fluent in several languages. She also began training as a nurse after leaving school at fifteen, but, once she had got enough money together, she changed vocation and trained to be an art teacher instead. From an early age, you know, I was also quite active in socialist groups, Lena confided, whilst carefully studying the reaction on my face, I was only about twenty and was soon heading up the women's division in my local region, she had added.

What she did not tell me that afternoon, was that she was carrying on those activities in this prison. Even here. Perhaps I did not quite have her trust at that stage. Later that evening Carl told me a little more about Lena.

My Lena, ah my Lena, he declared when he heard that I'd stumbled across her working with the infants, She really is a gem. Do you know how we met? Carl suddenly asked, We didn't meet here, you know, we came across each other briefly in the late thirties. Lena was already on a blacklist and had spent time in prison for distributing resistance leaflets. We had a joint friend and we came across one another one evening at her house. When we met again here, Lena had been arrested some months before under suspicion of assisting in a sabotage attack on an ammunition factory in Czechoslovakia. But, she did more than resistance work. Nothing could be proven against her, though, but instead of releasing her, they sent her here. She also looked after women and children whose husbands and fathers had already been arrested and deported. And she took food and clothes to the local prisons where they were held captive. A tireless worker, you know.

And her way of coping with all this, you may ask, continued Carl, Well, she simply does not accept it as a worthwhile reality. It's a very pragmatic approach. She expends no energy or emotions on it, instead all her energy and emotions are directed towards her children here, her resistance work and towards creating a better life in the future, and…Carl glanced mischievously towards me, And of course to her role as Greta, at which point Carl rolled onto his back, sighed a long drawn-out sigh and then laughed a hearty laugh, Do you know, she really is a wonderful Greta, he confided after several minutes of silence, Don't you agree?

~ ~ ~

The next distinct moment I remember is just after I had begun to work in the bakery. I remember it because it was so disturbing. I say disturbing, yet that is not what I remember feeling then. A few weeks of being at this place had numbed my senses. Unlike Carl, my experience of it did not make me more sensitive, more despairing of the world, and at the same time more giving. Not then. I became cold and gradually lost touch with my inner being. I became more like an automaton. I functioned. I thought little. I survived.

That is how I would describe my behaviour after the first few weeks. But it was to get worse. It was the incident in the bakery that should have served as a warning to me. That should have made me chide myself for my reactions, and for the eclipsing of my humanity.

I had been lucky enough to get one of the highly sought-after jobs in the bakery. Although the shifts were long, with a hundred or so of us to each shift, there was plenty of warmth and there were also opportunities for stealing bits of bread and other food stored there. It was Carl who had managed to get me the job soon after I'd arrived. One of the transports heading East had taken all inmates over seventy years old. Carl had been lucky. Carl's seventieth birthday was two days after this transport. A few of these older men had worked alongside Carl in the bakery and he quickly put my name forward as a replacement.

It was not very often that the guards bothered us in our work. They mostly stayed at their watch-posts at the perimeters of the camp and on the streets. But for some reason they were inspecting buildings on this particular day and arrived at the bakery quite early in the morning.

Within seconds of arriving, one particularly vigilant guard spotted a woman huddled near the ovens in a deep sleep. He didn't bother to warn her of his intentions. Instead, he just set about punching and kicking her. The woman was trying to protect her stomach as the guard continued to lash out at her in a frenzy of uncontrolled violence. I watched the guard beat up the woman for some minutes. I was not watching with a sense of pity, or with anger. I was not watching with some kind of sadistic pleasure, like some of the guards who were egging on the assailant. My emotions had been suspended. I was waiting for the perfect image…I was waiting for the kill, for after the kill… I knew that I could watch the woman being mauled and devoured bit by bit and would still be able to stand perfectly still. Unflinchingly still. Carl had also witnessed the scene. He'd been standing quite close to where the woman was sleeping. He had tried to lurch forward to assist her when he saw the guard pounce. My eyes had caught his just before he'd been ordered back to work by another guard. His eyes had wrenched me back to reality, as I saw a single tear role down his cheek. Fellow inmates hurried to the woman's rescue once the guards had left, but Carl had been unable to move. He had seen the blood between her legs. He had surmised in an instant that an unborn baby had been brutally murdered. Needlessly so.

There was no time to linger on the moment, on the tragedy. The funeral cart loaded up with bread was waiting to be pulled, and I, one of the stronger ones in the bakery, needed to be harnessed to it.

~ ~ ~

Usually I just put my head down and worked myself into a rhythm when pulling the cart. Today, I felt the need to look around this place again as I began to haul the cart which seemed heavier than usual. I needed to recapture the essence of it. In a detached way. I needed to feel again what I had first felt as I'd explored it on my very first day. On first arriving here in the middle of the night, and after having waited for hours in the central courtyard to be registered and deloused, I'd needed, like a cat, to discover the territory. To explore my surroundings. I had wanted to find Carl, but I had also wanted to find out what kind of place I'd landed in. I tramped around the grid-patterned streets from end to end, internalising all aspects. Internalising the symmetry. There were wide roads and narrower ones with a large square at the centre. It looked as though the prison had been a fort in the past and various administrative buildings were now housed in the barracks. Most of the buildings were two or three-storeys high and were similar in design. All were in a state of disrepair and dilapidation. There were three fortified and guarded gates, and through one of the gates I had also glimpsed a kind of small fortress some way off. It was only later that I would discover that this was where the solitary confinement cells, gallows and a plaza for the firing squad were hidden from view.

I had mapped out the place with my bed-roll still strapped around my back. Most of my other belongings had disappeared during the registration period. Looking back to my first day, I now realise that they were precious hours which I'd spent wandering. Not really belonging here, still feeling like a stranger in the midst of the misery and squalor, yet still registering it. The place was small – less than one square mile, and yet it had taken me hours to explore its streets and dwellings, and to work my way through the masses of people of all ages crammed inside it. I'd gone in and out of buildings and up and down the storeys of the barracks. There were women's, men's and children's barracks. There were barracks for the sick and elderly, there were barracks for the mentally ill. In the cellar of one of the women's barracks, I had stumbled across prison cells.

Each barrack block was divided into about a hundred rooms with many people housed in each one and occupying part of a bunk or a mattress on the floor as their own private space. Thousands seemed to have been assigned beds in one of the men's barracks, which also became my home.

I had felt so free on that bitter January afternoon. Or rather detached. I had been the camera eye, roving round the surroundings, capturing this or that image or scene, zooming in here and there and remaining motionless for minutes on end just staring. How different to now, how different to pulling this funeral cart along the streets. Harnessed to death, yet loaded with the bread of life.

The camera eye, the camera eye, I began to murmur under my breath, See through the lens, through the lens, I told myself, Detach, detach, I chanted doggedly to the rhythm of my dragging feet, Detach yourself, detach yourself, I continued to recite, until I felt my eyes widen and extend before me. I had trained my muscles well, and I still knew how to use my eye muscles in order to perceive my surroundings differently. It was as if the retina's structure changed shape with the chanting and with the stretching of the muscles. It was as if all the nerve-endings in my eyes had suddenly come alive again. My eyes gradually began to regain a depth and clarity of vision that, I now realise, had become increasingly contracted and blurred since arriving at the place. During the first weeks my eyes must have recoiled into themselves without my noticing. A kind of self-preservation mechanism that had caused the depth and scope of my vision to shrink. Perhaps in order to shield my mind from the reality of the place and to blinker me from my surroundings. From the hideous reality.

Now I suddenly saw myself as I must have been for the last few weeks — an ox tramping its well-trodden furrow up and down the sodden earth, shackled to its load and not seeing either side of it. I paused for a moment and turned my head half a circle to the left and then half a circle to the right. I held my eyes quite still as I did this, and moved my head slowly enough for my eyes to capture the scenes. For me to absorb the reality. For it to sink in.

Shadowy figures trudged down the mud-clotted and cobbled roads which were gradually turning into pools of quagmires on this wet morning. They were bent forward and were trailing their feet after them. Huddled in doorways and crouching at the sides of the road were a few elderly people. Some stretched their hands out to passers-by, others were so weak with hunger and infested with lice that they no longer had the strength or willpower to do even this. They just lay there slumped like ragged soiled heaps of flesh. Rats could also be seen scurrying between barracks, sniffing at the stagnant puddles of urine and excrement which had spilled out of buckets, on their way to the pits to be emptied.

In the lumberyard and the joiner's workshop inmates were hunched over planks of rough wood, busy constructing bits of furniture ordered by the guards, as well as secretly creating their own pieces of simple furniture as soon as the opportunity arose.

My eyes moved suddenly to the quarantine station. A buzz of activity just outside the doors caught my attention. A new outbreak of typhoid, no doubt, I thought to myself. More sick people than usual were being crammed into the building. Many lay on make-shift stretchers and wheelbarrows at the entrance waiting for a nurse to attend to them and to find a spare bunk. As I stared a little longer, I noticed a new arrival being carried towards the building. It looked as though it was the woman from the bakery. The main hospital building must have been full.

~ ~ ~

That evening I held my inaugural lecture. It was on photographic art and had been planned for some weeks. Carl, who had helped organise it and had put my name forward as soon as I arrived at the camp, did not turn up. It was only later that I was to learn that the woman in the bakery had been Carl's lover. That it was Lena. That the unborn child was theirs. It had been an unwritten rule between us not to talk about our personal tragedies. It was an unwritten rule among most inmates here.

That evening I spoke of the skills of a cameraman especially when photographing nature. I spoke with passion and conviction and with my absolute love of nature and, in so doing, managed to transport the eager audience to the wilderness of the Steppes. There were no seats available in the barracks and the audience stood for most of my talk. They stood, but they were also watching and studying the wildlife and nature with me, as I brought it to life with descriptions, sounds, and even impressions. Carl would have loved some of the anecdotes, I remember thinking, as I mimicked some of the animals and their idiosyncrasies.

I spoke of the cameraman's skills and of how it was necessary to disconnect the sensibility and to numb the heart and nerves in order to keep filming, even when an innocent animal was being torn apart. Even when minutes before my heart had expanded with aesthetic pleasure as I had watched this very same animal grazing peacefully on the plains, unaware of the fragility of the moment, of its brevity.

I then took the audience into the very heart of nature and spoke of the wondrous patterns and relations manifested in nature. With great enthusiasm and engagement I described many of the exotic insects, and especially butterflies which I had encountered on my travels and had tried to capture on film.

I spoke of how I had observed a butterfly unfolding its paper-thin wings for the very first time, and then watched it shake them dry. I spoke of how I had studied a bud as it gradually squeezed itself open over days. I talked of the energy contained within nature. Within that single bud. And how, only weeks before, the twigs had appeared shrivelled, arid and lifeless.

The audience hung onto my every syllable and pause. I was freeing up their minds to a different world. And for this they seemed grateful.

I had not been prepared for the intense reactions. I had forgotten how hungry we all were for such words and images. I, too, had pushed them back into the far recesses of my mind. Some inmates came up to me after the lecture and shook my hand. Moist eyes expressed what they could not rationally articulate.

I was there with you, one elderly man enthused in a hoarse voice, I could smell the cheetah's fur, I could see the slight twitch of her tautly-flexed muscles and every small dilation of her pupils. I could feel her strength. I could hear the grass whispering around her as it stroked her arched paws. I felt her concentration. I was there. For one brief moment, I was there.

As I turned to take my leave from the organiser of the lecture series, he gently slipped a portion of bread into my hand, and without hesitation, I eagerly grasped it and carefully tucked it into the inside of my jacket.

~ ~ ~

It was some time before Carl spoke to me. Carl was already in his bunk when I arrived back from the lecture. Rain was tapping lightly against the flimsy windows for most of the night, and we'd been lying in our bunks for several hours before I heard him quietly call across to me.

My friend, are you still awake? Are you listening to the night? Carl inquired in a faint husky whisper. I sensed that he knew that I was still awake. That he had been listening to me and not just to the night, that he'd been anticipating and following my thoughts. My thoughts about the lecture and about the audience's reaction to it.

Well, my friend, how did it go, he asked, and before waiting for my response, continued, Were you nervous? Did they ask lots of questions at the end of it? They usually do. Could you answer them?

Carl, I've not stopped thinking about it since, I replied. About life, about my time before and my time now. And, yes, to be honest, I did enjoy it. Strangely enough, I did. It wasn't just the audience which seemed to abandon itself to what I was saying, I, too, lost myself in the other world. The world that used to be. And what was so precious, was, that within that small space and that short period of time, our minds could meet beyond all this here. We were no longer inmates, brow-beaten and down-trodden and at the mercy of the whims of a brutal or sadistic overseer. We weren't miserable and suffering. We were free. We tasted together the freedom and the beauty of life. For the first time in a long while I feel content.

Treasure that feeling, my friend, I remember Carl telling me, Treasure it and keep it somewhere special inside you. Who knows, when you'll need it again. Make sure it's safe, but make sure you can find it when you need it. You will need it, my friend, believe me, and perhaps it will also find you when you're really down.

It was only then that I remembered the incident in the bakery that morning, that I remembered Carl's grief. Yet I couldn't mention it now. I'd missed the moment to ask Carl about it. Life had already moved on and his grief could no longer be shared. That much we both sensed. So we talked about literature instead, or rather, Carl, sensing perhaps my own thoughts, began to engage me in a reflection on Shakespeare and Goethe. Whereas I would try and distract him with animal antics and the camera's eye, Carl always resorted to Shakespeare when life became especially difficult.

What I like about Shakespeare, is that we don't know him, Carl suddenly stated. We don't know what he thought, we know little about his life. We try and work out who he was from his plays, poems and sonnets. But we'll never really know. He lived in an age where egos counted for little, except of course the egos of the rulers. With Goethe it's the opposite. I think Goethe wanted to be famous and knew how to cultivate fame. And of the two, there's no doubt that Goethe had the greater mind. He was truly a polymath. And we feel him everywhere in his work. And with Shakespeare we're not even sure what is truly his own work. The work is greater than his person. That's why it has lasted the test of time. That's why the work is so revered.

And Goethe's work? I inquired.

Goethe's work is less rounded, it can be easily fragmented, Carl continued, We can find so many gems in whole passages of reflection, prose or poetry, and for any and every occasion. Goethe was a great thinker, Shakespeare was first and foremost an actor. An actor in and with life. His work is full-bloodied. His work lives. And we can live with it. I live with it here. I live in it daily. Perhaps hourly, Carl chuckled as he glanced across to me before continuing, But with Goethe I reflect. I feel distance. A kind of distance from life. With Goethe I think about the inner make-up of individuals, and of course about my own. With Shakespeare I see it acted out before me, I get inside it, I act it out, I become.

It was good to hear Carl so engaged again. Still interested in his trade, in his love of life. That interest had not yet abandoned him. It was his hold on life, and it was his thoughts and ideas that he was able to communicate so well to the youngsters. And they knew it was genuine. It was not just learnt from books and from other people. It was lived through. It was felt.

And Goethe was right when he called Shakespeare's works a fairground – one big lively fairground, continued Carl, And a fast-moving fairground at that! Whereas Faust was written over decades, no, written is also the wrong expression, it was not written, just as Shakespeare's plays were not written, no, no, they evolved on the stage and from the acting and from the situation and relations at the time. From the world as he and the Elizabethans knew it. And Goethe's Faust also evolved. It evolved over time, over a lifetime, and so in Faust we are left with eternal ideas. Goethe's work, thinking and ideas of a lifetime flow into Faust.

Carl struggled to keep his voice going, as a fit of spluttering and wheezing overwhelmed him and also caused his straw mattress to rustle and his plank-bed to rattle. He rolled onto his side and then dragged himself up to a sitting position. He coughed and wheezed some more, as he struggled to light a candle stub carefully hidden by one of the legs of his bunk.

At that point I suddenly remembered the piece of bread I had carefully hoarded away in my inside pocket and, moving some clothes which were sprawled along a string fastened between the top bunk-beds, I reached over to Carl with it. Carl didn't want to take the bread at first. Still coughing and spluttering, he held one hand over his mouth, and with the other tried to gesticulate to me that I should keep it, that he couldn't take it from me. But I insisted. And as he chewed slowly on the hardened crust, his coughing gradually subsided.

I sat beside him on the bed. Carl was on the bottom row of the three-tier plank-bed. A few moans and groans from his neighbours above could be heard. They'd been disturbed by Carl's coughing. You could smell body close to body, the bruised and sore bodies. I'd been lucky to get a mattress and a bed to myself. Many of the younger ones who'd recently arrived were lying on the sawdust-covered floor, some without mattresses, and most with barely more than a metre of floor space to themselves. A few beds away from ours somebody was also mumbling what sounded like a prayer.

Carl remained unfazed by the groans and murmurings and continued as before, a little slower, however, and with gasps for breath between clusters of words, Perhaps another big difference, he declared, Is that Goethe actually accompanied the troops into battles. He witnessed for himself the bloodshed and politics of it all, perhaps that's why he rarely tries to capture it in a play, he's been too close to it, and it's too real for him. Whereas Shakespeare allows his imagination to work on the accounts he hears and reads, he lacks the brutal intimacy of it all and can use battles and warfare as a kind of abstraction, as a way of delving into the human psyche and into human relations. Carl halted. The flame of the tiny candle flickered, as if to fill the pause in Carl's thoughts with a quick twirl-like dance.

I closed my eyes momentarily and felt the blood flow softly through my veins. After a little while I opened them partly and gazed once more into the candle's flame. Then I closed the left eye completely and, keeping my right eye half open, I moved it up and down so as to create long thin beams of light which darted first upwards and then downwards from the flame, until I had adjusted my eyes so that the beam extended simultaneously in both directions. The quicker I moved my eye, the more dynamic the flame became. Carl, do you dream at night? Do you dream here? I asked after a while.

My friend, I have the most wonderful dreams, Carl quickly replied, Before they were quite trivial, no, trivial is the wrong word, they were often about the character I was playing. And so often, yes so very often my friend, they were about suddenly forgetting my lines in the middle of a performance. I couldn't help smiling at this point, and despite the dim light from the candle, the smile also didn't escape Carl.

You smile, my friend, and it's funny how unimportant those old dreams now seem. In my dreams here my mind expands in all kinds of ways. It's as if I experience my life for a second time, only this time differently and on a deeper level. I see friends and family again whom I've not seen for years or who have long since departed. When we meet in my dreams I have time for them, it's only now that I really appreciate them and the moments we shared together. A strange thing time. It's as if I'm now living that present time which is so long past, it is as if its essence has been delayed and it is now fulfilling a secret purpose, as if it'd been deliberately stored for the future. And I now have the conversations with the loved ones that I couldn't have then. Past, present, future time – my friend, these have taken on new meanings here. Before I was always thinking of the future when I should have been enjoying the present, now I find that the present comes to me from the past, and I can experience it new, feel it differently and that gives me hope for the future.

I know what you're saying, Carl, I too felt that tonight, when I gave my lecture. It was as if I were back on the Steppes, back in the wilderness, only this time I was more intensely there. Every nerve in my body was suddenly alive. And this time I could feel consciously that which I'd perhaps unconsciously absorbed back then. And when I get out of here, Carl, I know I'll experience everything differently again. And it doesn't have to be the Steppes. It doesn't have to be so exotic. A woodland. Any old woodland. And any old woodland will no longer be any old woodland. It no longer is in my mind. In my mind I now see and feel the woods I've always known in a new way.

And you have yet to know our little wood here, Carl intervened in a gentle voice, When you arrived winter was already upon us. You didn't see the blossom, you didn't see the autumn colours or smell their richness. You didn't see the few golden dandelions dancing at the chestnut trees' feet. We have only a few trees in our wood, and to call them a wood is a bit of an exaggeration. But they're so precious, I have even given each one of them names and have adopted them as part of my family. And with this, Carl let out a little chuckle, But, you know what, I think many others have done the same, and now Carl laughed out loud and, for a moment, completely forgot all about his sleeping companions.

Sometimes I lie under my trees when the guards are not watching, Carl whispered, As I lie looking upwards it seems that the tree possesses a never-ending height, that life goes on and on, branching this way and that and reaching ever upwards, way beyond my view and into infinity. And I wonder why painters don't try and capture this horizontal perspective on life. I look up into the trees and to the skies and it's as if I am floating. I no longer care. I dissolve into the never-ending Universe and am no longer here.

A long pause followed, as Carl turned once more to lie on his back, and began to stare at the wooden planks above him until he gradually lost himself in his thoughts, and seemed to forget about my presence. I watched the candle flame flutter, then contract into a tiny ball of light before suddenly extending upwards with a new burst of energy. I watched for some time as the flame waved and twirled to and fro, almost disappearing and then sparking up again, until I heard Carl softly chant, The stars above us govern our conditions, else one self mate and make could not beget such different issues. He'd gone back to his Shakespeare.

Yet, I didn't want our chat to end, But how will we experience all this here when it too becomes part of our past, how will you experience it all, Carl, I persisted.

Ah, my friend, the mind can do wonderful things, that much my acting has taught me. But will you, my friend, still be fascinated by the power and violence of nature as you were before, that is the real question? My friend, there's beauty everywhere, even here. You laugh scornfully and perhaps don't believe me, but you captured it tonight, and your audience felt it. Is that not so?

But I can't find beauty in killing, not in senseless murder, not in a wondrous life needlessly extinguished. My friend, in finding that beautiful, we betray life. Death is part of life, killing is part of life, it's part of nature, it happens, I know that's what you're going to tell me. But, when it happens needlessly or cruelly, I still can't find that beautiful. The sadness I feel eclipses any sense of beauty. My friend, it's the beautiful and noble images that fill my dreams here. These are the images that I now need.

I hear what you're saying, Carl. But before I could say more, the stillness of the night was already coming to an end, and even before the sky had lightened, the first marchers of the morning were beginning their tramp through the streets and out to their labour sites on the outskirts of the prison.

The next thing I heard was the early morning sirens and the supervisor of our section ordering us out of our beds. And soon the barracks had become one heaving mass of chaos with bodies moving in all directions and shouting and grunting at each other and jostling one another out of the way, as men hurried to the adjacent washroom before stumbling into their clothes and then bundling together their sparse belongings, ready for a new day.

Today did not proceed, however, in the usual way. In the way that I had grown accustomed to since being here. Soon after getting up, the atmosphere began to change in the place. There was a definite frisson of excitement. Not quite visible, not at first, but definitely in the air. And as I began my round of delivering the bread, I noticed tins of paint being unloaded from a van and deposited near the main square. Soon trucks delivering all sorts of materials began to arrive. As I turned another corner I saw small groups of people busy hammering together pieces of wood near one of the main streets. They appeared to be constructing benches.

You're not going to believe this, Carl, I said, on my return to the bakery, I think this place is having a face-lift. Do you have any idea what's going on? Have you heard any rumours?

Oh plenty of rumours, plenty of those already, this place is full of them, began Carl and laughed out loud, We were hoping though that you'd be able to tell us more, that you'd have seen what it's all about on your rounds. We were relying on you, my friend, Carl teased.

Well, I can certainly tell you that buildings in the main street are being painted and benches are being constructed. I even saw trucks bringing in soil, but I've no idea why it's all happening. Neither had the inmates doing the work. Perhaps this place is going to become a spa-town after all, I joked.

A few days later I was able to report some more. Near the old town hall, it looked as though clusters of inmates were planting flowers and laying a lawn. Another few days passed and an ornamental park appeared. As if by magic. Suddenly the scent of late spring blossoms permeated the air. When I recounted this latest development to Carl, he became especially excited.

We're not allowed to use the park though, Carl, I quickly added, trying to distil any immediate thoughts he may have of relaxing on one of the newly constructed benches, But, if you go there after work, you'll be able to smell the flowers, you'll see the colours now dotted all about. It's quite something.

A few days after this, I noticed building work taking place along some of the wider streets. Cafes and façades were being erected. A music pavilion was also being assembled. Carl was quite unsurprised when I told him all this, and mentioned new rumours about special visitors coming to the place. He'd also heard from several performing groups that certain productions had been ordered by the guards. The guards themselves did not, however, seem to know much about it all, but had transmitted the orders to the necessary groups, as had been required.

Was Faust going to be affected, I remember asking Carl. Were they likely to lose more of their actors? They'd already lost several to transports over the past few months. Luckily, Lena had so far not been amongst them. At one point it looked as though she very nearly could have been when more lists were being drawn up for deportations of the infirm.

Lena had been sick for some time following the beating in the bakery. Several of her ribs and upper thigh-bone had been broken and she'd suffered a serious internal infection which had lingered on for many weeks. Antibiotics were in extremely short supply, and for weeks on end they had been non-existent. She'd hovered between life and death at one point, especially when she also succumbed to the typhoid epidemic that suddenly spread through the place, taking hundreds of lives in its wake. Sheer willpower and the need to get back to her orphans had pulled her through.

Many of the young children had visited her whilst she'd been in the hospital. They brought her cards they'd made from scraps of paper and a few pressed flowers, and they told her about some of the fairytales which they'd continued to invent in her absence.

Mara, a friend of Lena's, had stood in for Lena, and had continued to play with the younger children in the way that Lena used to every afternoon. She also stood in for her early morning shift at the bakery so that Lena did not lose this job to one of the other inmates. Such jobs were highly coveted.

For Lena the job was not so much about the extra rations of bread. Nor was it particularly about the warmth during the long winter months. Lena was involved in clandestine resistance activities and had managed to keep these going via the bakery and the delivery of bread. Mara, just turned twenty-one, was also part of the women's resistance group. She, too, had knowledge of the secret code that Lena placed in loaves of bread, whenever she got an opportunity to do so, and which she then discretely marked. It had become my job to ensure that these particular loaves of bread reached the right inmates.

~ ~ ~

My friend, I had the most wonderful dream last night, Carl whispered to me from his bunk, once most of the inmates were already sleeping, It began in a pasture of vibrant yellow flowers. A soft carpet of blossom embroidered with every shade of yellow you can imagine, and more beyond the imagination. Carl cast a mischievous glance in my direction as he uttered this last phrase, checking to see whether I was listening to him. I was, and responded with a smile.

There were thousands upon thousands of individual yellow flowers. But it wasn't just the meadow that was yellow. When I looked up to the sky, the sky was laced with threads of gold. Every shade of gold you can imagine with sunlight weaving in and out of the threads. And the threads were all different in length, width and texture. Some appeared to be studded with translucent beads which shone and glittered in irregular patterns, and winked at me and mesmerised me. I kept on gazing around, trying to absorb the treasure trove of shades and shapes and chasing the droplets of sunshine in between. After some time, a fine line of continuous orangey-red light began to emerge on the distant horizon. As the light expanded, I gently rose to my feet and made my way towards it in a trance-like state.

With every step I took, I became lighter, the air around me seemed to get warmer and the scents of the flowers became more intense. The flowers soon began to change into thousands of shades of orange, as did the sky above me. I kept on walking until everything around me had turned red. And then, caressed by such warmth and heady with such vibrancy of colour, I lay down once more on the carpet of flowers and fell into a heavenly slumber.

Carl, whose eyes had been transfixed to the wooden planks of the bunk-beds above him, turned his head towards me. He wanted to see if I was still with him in his dream. I was. When I awoke, Carl announced after some moments, I was back in the yellow field.

I watched him for a while, expecting him to continue. He didn't. He hadn't just awoken in his dream, he had also woken from it.

The silence hung in the air for what must have been a long time, although it didn't really feel long. Carl seemed to want to savour the beauty of his dream and had no need of talk. I allowed the dream to warm his senses for a moment, before I jokingly added, Ah, Carl, you've been spending too much time with those newly planted flowers, they're sending you crazy, that's what is happening. As Carl turned towards me, I could see his lightly closed mouth twitch at the edges before he responded with a generous smile and a twinkle in his eye.

A few weeks later, and after one of our many rehearsals with the youngsters, Carl recounted a similar dream to me again. My friend, remember my wonderful colourful dream which I told you about some weeks back. I remembered it as vividly as Carl had first recounted it to me, and nodded affirmatively. Well, my friend, my dream continued last night. I was back in that magical field of colour and scent. I was languishing amongst the luxurious softness and warmth of it all and I felt so incredibly rich and content. And as I breathed in slowly and deeply, every vein in my body began to expand, eagerly absorbing as much colour and perfume as possible. It was truly intoxicating.

And after a while I gazed up to the sky. Only this time when I scanned the sky, a chink of green light began to appear on the horizon. I once again rose gently to my feet and set off towards the promise of green hues. Gradually, step by step, thousands of shades of green emerged and expanded before my eyes and under my feet. I walked and walked for hours on end, or so it seemed, and the air became cooler. Then all of a sudden everything turned blue.

There had been no gradual transition, as in my first dream, and I was now encased in a blueness which was rapidly refracting into hundreds of shades of blue. When I looked towards my feet, I realised that there was no longer a meadow for me to rest my head. The pasture had turned to water and I was surrounded by floating foam-flowers. The water was getting higher and higher. But it didn't seem to matter. The water was a peaceful and caressing sensation. It lapped soothingly against my body. And as I kept on moving, I was no longer walking but floating. I was floating in a downwards direction, and I was going deeper and deeper into a fantastical ocean-world.

Carl paused and looked across at me. His eyes perused my face in one continuous flowing movement. Yes, I was still following him, that much he could see.

I was entering deeper into a world of natural rhythm and sound, Carl continued, A world of perpetually undulating swirling rhythms. And the sounds alternated in length and intensity. Sometimes they were very close, and then distant, and then close again. Sometimes they were deep and elongated, then they became short, pointed and high-pitched. Single sounds became merged with others, until there was a whole orchestra of wondrous sound which gradually built up to a climax and then gently faded away into the distance.

Fish of fantastical colours brushed against me. They squeezed between my legs, gently stroking my skin as they did so. Some lingered, some nudged at my body. Others seemed to want to drift along with me and stayed by my side for a while. And then there were the ones which tried to nibble at my skin and hairs. More out of curiosity than a desire to feed. At least, that's what it felt like. It was your world, my friend, Carl suddenly stated in an altogether different tone. It was a world of magical creatures, and I was captivated by every single one of them. Perhaps I will draw them for you one day, Carl suggested quite perkily, and perched himself up on one elbow to look at me properly. His eyes scanned my face several times, quizzically searching out every nerve and chain of muscular reaction.

Then Carl resumed his narrative and his gaze returned once more to the planks above him, Time had been completely suspended, as had space and weight. I no longer breathed as before, and when I looked towards my feet, I noticed that they too had become transformed into an exuberant tail that fluttered delicately through the currents. Instead of arms I now possessed fins and feathery gills. I also didn't see in the same way as before. I now saw with a different sense of perspective. I saw finer. I perceived colours and detail that I couldn't begin to describe to you now, my friend. I sensed, but could not see, that my head too must be an altogether different shape.

As I descended further I passed through a cascade of plants and floating flowers which were bobbing and swaying in rhythms of their own. I could feel the water around me becoming warmer, and I seemed to be entering an underwater oasis of thermal currents. Eventually I arrived at a kind of city. And the city was a labyrinth of luminous caves and caverns with spectacular arches, domes and peaks with lace-like corals and shells adorning the labyrinth. And chalices had been etched out of parts of the labyrinth. Delicate floating chalices, in which eggs of many colours lay hidden. Eggs that would bring forth new life. And it was as if the city were in constant motion with the plants which enveloped it. It was as if the whole city were dancing. My friend, that is what it felt like, and I, too, danced to the strange rhythms of this magical world, and I too was free.

At this point, Carl broke off from his dream. It would be some time before he returned to it.

~ ~ ~

The night before the long-awaited visit, Carl engaged me in a discussion once more about Hamlet. Carl had not gone to his bed immediately when the lights had gone out, but instead had hovered at the window and was trying to breathe in the sultry midsummer night air through a crack in one of the panes. I watched him for some time, studying his outline and his breathing. His posture was still well disciplined despite his shrunken stature, I remember thinking.

Hamlet, my friend, he murmured in a low voice after I had joined him at the window, Is all about play, about plays and playing within plays.

Playing plays, playing madness, playing at sword-fighting, clowns playing grave-diggers, and so it goes on. And yet, the poison lurks beneath it all, even if it is hidden from view or disguised. The poison that is rotting the land, its people and its very foundations is just waiting for its moment to erupt and turn the court into a gruesome carnage.

Carl halted his narration, inhaled the balmy air once more, and then continued, It's not really about Hamlet's delay in avenging his father's murder. The fraternal murder has already happened before the play begins, and so the country's foundations have already been poisoned. And in the end just about everybody has drunk of it, and has been infected in some way or other, so great is the pus-oozing wound and the rottenness, Carl declared in a measured way but with a trace of premonition in his voice.

And this wound had to be lanced, the poison had to come to the surface in order for the source of the vile infection to be stemmed. Some more minutes passed before Carl resumed, this time, however, his voice was lighter and tinged with a hint of forthrightness, So, my friend, Goethe was right about Germany being Hamlet. But for the wrong reasons. In fact, Goethe probably unwittingly harmed Germany by suggesting that there is an affinity between the essence of Germanness and the figure of Hamlet who suffers from the weight of history. Not that Goethe actually said that. But that was how it came to be interpreted. It was Goethe, you know, who first took Hamlet out of the context of Shakespeare's drama, and gradually Hamlet turned more and more into a cult figure, until eventually Germany becomes Hamlet and the figure of Hamlet becomes a key player without the strength of nerve that forms a hero.

Carl laughed a bitter laugh, before continuing, And now, in order for Germany to prove that it is no Hamlet, that it is heroic, it has turned into this monster. This foul putrid pus-oozing monster. Germany is Hamlet the play because its foundations have been so utterly poisoned. And now we, too, are to become a myth. A play within a play ordered by the Germans. A play of pretence, and of make-believe that all is well here in this castle of depraved containment.

But, my friend, continued Carl in an altogether stronger and determined voice, and before I could offer any kind of response, By putting on our own secret play within the play of this play, it is for us, too, to be as cunning as Hamlet was with Claudius, his blood-uncle and blood-stained usurper of a king. Carl paused slightly, inhaled deeply, then continued in a commanding voice, We'll put on the act of pretence, of pretending all is well, yet we'll allude to the poison, we'll bring it to the surface, We must! As Carl hurled these fighting words into the heavy night air, he grabbed hold of my shoulder and squeezed it hard, then pulled me close to his side before patting me gently on the back a couple of times and sighing a long slow sigh.

I sensed that Carl did not want or expect me to respond. He needed to voice his private thoughts and fears. It was not my role to contradict or counter them or upset his own inner logic and balance.

~ ~ ~

They're heading this way, I furtively called to Carl from outside of the room of the freshly painted barrack, There's a small entourage, the guards are also with them, so is the Commandant.

I'd been hanging around the building for some time, keeping watch, whilst pretending to be digging out weeds from the newly-planted flower-beds. Carl was inside with the youngsters. They were pretending to have one of their usual training sessions, only this one would be different. Timing was of the essence, as was gesture, intonation and emphasis. Not for play, not for fun as in the other sessions. We all realised that our audience's mind needed to be nudged in a certain direction. That part of the audience would be listening differently from the other, at least that's what we hoped. We knew that we would have only one chance to get it right. There would be no other performances.

My friend, We are all to be Hamlets, I remember Carl having announced the previous evening once we'd returned to our beds. He'd chuckled at this sudden insight, and then had mischievously added, You, my friend, the one who never wanted to act, you now have your greatest role. I remember Carl giving me a quizzical look, smiling, before resting his head back on his mattress. Then in a voice full of affected and playful pathos he had declared, The time is out of joint. O cursed spite that ever I was born to get it right!

After some moments he lifted his head, turned once more towards me and, in an altogether quiet and serious voice had whispered, My friend, our method must expose this madness, this Hell, we must get it right, we must. Carl had been referring to the much anticipated visit by the International Red Cross.

It was these words and the timbre of his voice which now rang in my head as I watched the visitors slowly approach. Inside, Carl was busy directing the youngsters to their positions. Most of this was accomplished with a deft hand movement. The scene had been rehearsed. We'd been rehearsing it for weeks. The youngsters knew the

Act inside out and were poised ready to begin. They began in the middle. They began in such a way that it looked as though they'd been working through the play to this point, to this crucial point.

As soon as the heavy footsteps could be heard, Sam, a young lad of thirteen, thrust back his shoulders, extended his neck, and declared, There's the respect that makes calamity of so long life, for who would bear the whips and scorns of time. Just as Carl had rehearsed with him, Sam slightly overemphasised the word 'whips' and paused for a second after uttering the word 'scorns'. Not too long to make it obvious, but long enough hopefully to draw attention to the words.

Had the visitors noticed? Had they been listening to the words? Listening in a certain way? It was hard to tell. They displayed little emotion. Sam continued, Th' oppressor's wrong, the proud man's contumely, the pangs of disprized love, the law's delay, the insolence of office, and the spurns that patient merit of th'unworthy takes, when he himself might his quietus make with a bare bodkin?

At this point, Carl interrupted and suggested Sam try the passage again, and Carl spoke the lines for him with a different emphasis and rhythm. Sam experimented with the new rhythm, pretending to be learning the part and learning from Carl. And Carl pretended to be listening to him for the first time, Who would these fardels bear, to grunt and sweat under a weary life, but that the dread of something after death, the undiscovered country east from whose bourn no traveller returns, puzzles the will, and makes us rather bear those ills we have than fly to others that we know not of?

Did they notice? Was it loud enough? Did they know their Shakespeare? Did they notice the slight change? The small inserted word spoken very quickly and softly so that it was scarcely perceptible. Did they understand what we meant, what we wanted them to understand? Anna playing Ophelia picked up her cue and she and Sam entered into a quick exchange, to which Carl suggested a few different gestures.

Ah yes, this Germanic drama! This great Germanic drama, declared one of the guards accompanying the visitors, In Hamlet we find a piece of our true selves, a weakness, which we as true Germans must overcome. You know, Hamlet, in the end, also realises the need for action, the guard continued, Unfortunately, for him it is too late, his strength comes to him too late. We have learnt Hamlet's lesson well. He smiled knowingly at his guests and then led them swiftly away.

Carl stared at the doorway long after they had all disappeared through it, and, then in a barely audible and resigned tone, he mumbled, Our life is a myth, like this play, this play is a myth like our life here, what is the difference? All the world's a stage.

He then collapsed to his knees and buried his head deep in his lap. It was some time before the inmates, who were crowded into the rooms above the first floor and well hidden from view and earshot of the visitors, dared to move.

~ ~ ~

Carl was right. He was right to sense that I had made a pact with myself. But, for once he was wrong about the timing. It was not until after the visit that I had vowed to take revenge. And it had been the sight of the thousands upon thousands of young and old lives being herded into cattle trucks that had set the matter for me in stone. I became of stone. I became of stone after witnessing the relentless march of the innocent in the direction of death. And I could do nothing. Absolutely nothing to stop it. They really did exist. The gas chambers. The rumours had had currency. Hard currency. Currency unlimited. Carl knew. He knew long before most.

My friend, do you think about what is beyond this Hell? Carl had asked me one night, but had not waited for a reply. I know what awaits us, he said, An even greater Hell, one beyond all imagination. And why, because it's so anchored in reality. In the perfect plan. You see, my friend, I've been reflecting, and it's been there all the time, the signs, the actions, the statements, the policy changes are there for all to see. But they've happened by increment. They've crept up on us all. And now the big mad plan is being acted upon. But most can't see it, so perfect is its execution, so insidious is its concept. So cleverly disguised. My friend, I've seen through the Act, I've worked out the plot, I know how it will end.

I didn't respond. Carl was uttering thoughts that I had been trying to suppress. I, too, had been thinking along similar lines. The fact that we didn't have families had perhaps freed up our minds. We had allowed ourselves to think the impossible, we had reconstructed the bigger picture. I, though, refused to dwell upon it.

~ ~ ~

My friend, I want to tell you about the dream I had the other night. I need to tell you about it although it is quite different to the other one, and I'm not really sure what to make of it. I wasn't so sure that I wanted to hear it. Carl's voice sounded heavy and troubled, yet undeterred.

It began once again with the yellow pasture, and then with my gentle descent into the ocean. Once again I saw the wondrous creatures. Once again I became part of their world. Once again I marvelled at the sea-city hidden within the oasis. Only this time I had taken on a different shape to last time. I was no longer a fish, but rather some kind of sea creature. Long tendrils hung from my many legs and appeared to propel me through the water.

But the fish surrounded me as before, some lingering longer than others, some brushing past me on their way to feeding grounds. Then I noticed fish arrive with strange markings on their backs. I say strange, because the markings were like letters of the alphabet, only bits of the letters were missing. I felt that it was my task to work out the missing bits. I sensed that the markings were messages. I sensed that it was up to me to decipher them, as the fish circled round me and tried to catch my attention.

I began to follow the fish, trying hard to keep them in view and to make sense of the shapes of words. I was trying to penetrate their secret. The secret of the fish. Once they realised that I was following them, they began to swim with a sense of urgency and I was finding it increasingly difficult to keep up.

We were now entering a different part of the ocean-world. Suddenly a cavernous trench opened before us and we were swept downwards by a powerful current. The waters around us became muddy with decay and excrement and freezing cold. Slimy substances like bladderwrack and dark green algae were floating all around us. Sharp crags of rock jutted out of the sides of the trench and occasionally pierced our skin. It was as if they were jaws staked with rows and rows of teeth and at any moment they would snap shut. I began to feel claustrophobic and threatened. We seemed to be descending into the hellish yawn of a giant ocean and tumbling our way through tortuous channels. The water became darker, stiller and so bitterly cold. The pressure increased and the sound of a haunting horn approached us from afar.

This journey seemed to last a life-time and with each stage of the journey, creatures of the deep increased in size and began to take on the form of gigantic sea monsters. Many were crouched on barely perceptible ledges. Others were trampling through the murky waters. Soon I began to smell what I thought was sulphur and the water began to get hotter. I saw little sparks of fire, and it was as if smoke were beginning to rise up from beneath us. Finally we arrived at the place to which the fish had wanted to lead me. To what looked like an underwater graveyard. And I suddenly found myself amongst millions of bones. Human bones. Children's. And all around us tongues of fire leapt out from under the seabed and stretched high above us.

Carl didn't look at me when he paused this time. Instead his eyes appeared to be almost clinging to the boards of the bunk-bed above him. His eyes were tense and wide open, and were welling up with water. I dared hardly breathe as I watched Carl and waited for him to resume his narration.

I stayed amongst the bones for some time, continued Carl in a slightly broken voice, And it was a while before I realised that the bones were encased by a giant sea monster. A squid-like serpent. Its multiple eyes of many shapes were pointing in different directions and its massive tentacles were everywhere. A sticky black substance was oozing from the insides of the tentacles and slowly creeping over the bones. As the substance inched nearer to where I was resting, I began to panic. I, too, could become a prisoner of this infernal monster, I remember thinking.

It was at this point that the mysterious fish reappeared. And now I could read the messages on their backs. Quite clearly. Only, now I didn't want to understand what I read, as the fish were urging me to enter the monster's mouth. If I entered the mouth, I could release the bones, that's how I interpreted their code. I could save the children. That was what I read.

I hesitated. I watched the fish again. I saw the message. I saw it as before. And this time I followed them. Upwards. For what seemed an eternity. Towards the head. Eventually we reached the mouth-like opening. Huge in circumference. And, without any further hesitation, I took a deep breath and propelled myself straight into it.

Now Carl did look at me. Or at least he turned his gaze towards me and scanned my face, yet his thoughts were still miles away. They were in the black hole into which he had descended and from which he was unable to escape.

And, my friend, Carl quietly resumed after a while, It was you who saved me. As I struggled in the darkness, in the claustrophobic enclosure in which I was being relentlessly pummelled and pushed in all directions by the motions of its throat, I saw you appear with a big sword in your hands and you began to hack at the monster's head. It took you some time, but eventually you managed to chop it off, and I swam free.

Carl hesitated for some moments before resuming, But when I looked behind me, I saw that all the bones were still trapped and vicious tongues of fire were leaping higher than ever all around them. I had failed to release the bones. The children had not been saved. And, to my horror, I also saw the monster's head gradually reappearing. Not just one. Now several seemed to be sprouting out of its body. The monster had grown more powerful than ever, and each new head was demanding more lives.

Carl glanced across at me, searched intensely into my eyes before continuing with his dream, And you, my friend, you were still trying desperately hard to fight all these heads, when I awoke once more.

Carl didn't want to end his tale on a sombre note and, after a few minutes, he joked, Do you know what my friend, I think I found myself right in the middle of Shakespeare's inspiration for King Lear, Yes, that's it, that's definitely it, that's what this dream was all about. Strange. Yes, but that's it. I was King Lir, the ocean god of early Irish legend, that's who I was.

Carl, if only, I replied, as I stretched out my fingers towards him and lightly brushed his shoulder. And we both looked at each other, though neither of us really managed to smile.

Can you believe it, my friend, I live another day? I've amazed myself by my own acting abilities. I fooled them. I actually fooled them, Carl whispered as he tugged at my jacket sleeve. They took me for a much younger man. The readiness is all, my friend, Hamlet was right. The rumour was also right, the rumour which I've been hearing for years, he hushed, If you look healthy and fit enough you survive… Well, you survive the first test, he added even more quietly, Do you know, I think that extra bit of sugar Lena gave me also did the trick. It perked me up no end.

Carl had miraculously survived the selection process on arrival at the death camp by remembering his Hamlet, the way he always used to play him in his younger days and by adopting the gait and mannerisms of the young prince. As we waited near the rail trucks in our rows of five men abreast, Carl was still puffing out his chest and extending his neck, with his chin pointed upwards. He was so preoccupied with his acting talent that he appeared not to notice the fate of the many hundreds now being herded off in a different direction.

At the right moment, you found the right role, Carl, I rejoined after a little while, pulling my patchwork jacket tightly around my body, You nearly fooled me. I couldn't help thinking, however, as we shuffled along in our rows, whether Carl would be able to sustain his newly found youth whilst out on hard labour to which we had now both been assigned.

The place we'd just left was nothing compared to this, I reflected, as I stared at the lines of huts stretching out before my eyes. The late autumn sun did little to distort my perspective. Nor Carl's, once his rush of adrenalin had subsided. We knew this place was going to be very different. We didn't say so. We didn't talk about it, instead we talked about Hamlet. Carl's Hamlet which had eclipsed the initial madness of this place, if only briefly. The method was deliberate. Shakespeare was Carl's survival technique. It was his way of diverting our attention from some of the horror, it had always been his way, and he'd just used it again to great effect. He'd never really needed my animal antics to distract him – that was my own self-delusion.

Carl's strategy was not one of self-deception. Carl knew only too well that the signs were ominous. And as I now overheard him muttering some of Hamlet's lines under his breath, I realized that he had sized up this new place in an instant. In one philosophical insight. There's a special providence in the fall of a sparrow, I heard him murmur, If it be now, 'tis not to come, if it be not now, yet it will come, the readiness is all, he stressed once more, only this time with a slight sense of resignation in his voice and with a bowed head, Since no man has aught of what he leaves, what is't to leave betimes. Then Carl fell silent.

~ ~ ~

Had I been prepared for this day, I now ask myself many years later? Had what I'd already witnessed of a Hell on earth prepared me for my own role in it? Why had I carried it out so perfectly?

I remember Carl was being particularly playfyl that day. Our work in the quarry was less arduous than usual because the lorries that normally carried away the gravel and stone had not turned up. We were too new to these work camps to realise that this could be a dangerous period for prisoners, especially for prisoners who had sadistic overseers. We were in quite high spirits as rumours had already begun to circulate that the lorries had been attacked and the prisoners were soon to be liberated. Some were even whispering that they'd heard the artillery fire and swore that our liberators were already on the doorstep. That made us even more giddy.

Carl decided he was going to engage me in some playful banter and began to quote some lines from Shakespeare, coaxing me into joining in with him. If music be the food of love, he suddenly turned to me and stated, and allowed the word 'love' to hang in the air, waiting for me to complete the line, Play on, I chirpily added, Give me excess of it, I enthused jokily, That surfeiting…, but before I could continue after my pregnant pause, Carl rejoined, The appetite may sicken and so die.

Carl closed his eyes and savoured the word 'die' with its full Shakespearian meaning, with the complete satiation of a lover after an orgasmic conclusion. He then took a deep breath, smiled, looked me up and down, before continuing in a dreamy-like voice and with his eyes diverted towards a distant point on the horizon, I know a bank where the wild thyme blows, where oxlips and the nodding violet grows, quite overcanopied with luscious woodbine, with sweet musk-roses, and with eglantine. I took the cue, it was for me to change this beautiful dream into one of debased lustfulness. I knew the way the mood shifted, There sleeps Titania sometime of the night, I continued, Lulled in these flowers with dances and delight, and there the snake throws her enamelled skin, weed wide enough to wrap a fairy in, and the juice of this I'll streak her eyes, and make her full of hateful fantasies.

Ah, that's too simple, my friend, Carl proclaimed, far too simple, the chant-like rhythm of these couplets brings forth the lines too easily, the lyrics you remember well. Too well. Let me test you with some more, O my offence is rank, it smells to heaven. It hath the primal eldest curse upon't. This time I did not wait for any kind of pause, before I interjected, A brother's murder. But, before I could continue, Carl had taken up Hamlet's uncle's speech once more, Pray I can not, though inclination be as sharp as will, my stronger guilt defeats my strong intent. Now it was my turn to interrupt him, And like a man to double business bound, I stand in pause where I shall first begin, and both neglect. Yet, it was Carl who was determined to have the final say and influence our mood, and so he swiftly moved the scene from Denmark to Venice, The quality of mercy is not strained. It droppeth as the gentle rain from heaven upon the place beneath. It is twice blessed, it blesseth him that gives and him that takes.

What we had failed to perceive in our playfulness was that one of the guards had been watching us. He must have been watching us for some time before he began to make his way towards us. He'd been harassing prisoners who were queuing up for the latrines. Unfortunately for us, he did not share our heightened spirits. We had only recently joined this working unit, yet he already appeared to have taken a distinct dislike to Carl. Perhaps he knew him to have been a well-known actor. Perhaps it was Carl's previous successes on the stage which so irked him.

It was already too late when I spotted him out of the corner of my eye, just as Carl was uttering the word 'blesseth'. I knew we were in deep trouble and I had tried to signal this to Carl. Carl, however, had his back to the guard and did not see him approaching. He did not see him flicking his whip with his right hand and allowing it gently to vibrate in his left. The guard walked in a measured way towards us, savouring each step whilst agitating the whip with increasing vigour, his eyes already working on the punishment which he was going to mete out on us. His reputation towered before him. Fearfully so. And yet Carl still had not noticed the change in my reaction, so engaged was he in his mercy speech.

You filthy dog! was all I remember the guard shouting, as he struck Carl across the back of his head, before turning his whip then on me. So fierce was the guard's first swipe at Carl that part of his scalp now hung loosely from the back of his head. Carl instinctively lifted his hand to his head to try and stem the blood, and to keep the hanging flesh attached. This earned him another whip from his torturer. Carl stumbled forwards. Instinctively, I reached out towards him to help him to his feet. That was another fatal mistake on that fateful day. On seeing the care we showed one another and our closeness, an even more sadistic side of the guard manifested itself.

So you two really care for each other, do you? He snarled at us through his heightened anger, That's nice, he continued as he allowed his wrath to subside before he carefully channelled it into an altogether different emotion, Real nice, that is. You talk Shakespeare together, that's very nice, he added. You act it out together, I'm told. That's good...Really good. Then there was a silence which froze the air and seemed to last for minutes. Although we both hung our heads quite low, I raised my eyes ever so slightly to try and catch sight of what the guard might be thinking. He appeared to be studying us, his eyes slowly rolled from side to side and began to narrow as he stared intently at us, yet his mind was evidently elsewhere. I'd like to see you act some more, right here, right now, just for me.

Neither of us dared say anything, but just nodded faintly with our heads and kept our eyes firmly focused on the ground. We could tell from his tone that there was more to this than the guard was revealing, Well, now, what's my favourite play? Ah, let me think a little…

I could tell from his voice that he already knew what he was going to say and what he had in mind for us. Yet, we were still in the dark. We were now his playthings. King Lear, yes, that's it, that's the play I'd like you to act out. A proper tragedy, that is, lots of love and hatred in it. We stood in complete silence, not daring to look at one another and not daring to utter a word. But let me see, the guard continued after another few moments of silence, What scene should it be? Now what's my favourite one? Why I know, the most gruesome one, of course. It has to be the one in which Lear's faithful Duke, or was it his Earl, gets blinded. Yes, that's the scene I'd like you to perform…properly mind. Authentically.

My mouth dried up in an instant, and my jaw seemed to lock in a half open position. I sensed Carl slightly shudder after the guard had uttered these words. I'll leave it to you to decide who plays the faithful Duke, the guard sneered gleefully.

Without a moment's hesitation, Carl immediately gestured that he would play Gloucester. I tried to protest, and turned to Carl to plead with him. It was then that I noticed that Carl's face had become ashen and he suddenly appeared ten years older. I felt violently sick at the thought of what was to come. Somehow I managed to contain the retching of my stomach by squeezing the muscles in my throat and neck as tightly as I possibly could. A cold sweat broke out on my forehead, and I felt each bead of salty liquid trickle slowly round my eyes and down my cheeks under my chin and to my jacket below. When I looked across at Carl, he quickly returned the glance with eyes that spoke a million words, as he saw me fight back the tears forming in mine.

No, Carl, I whispered under my breath, no I can't do it. The guard saw my reluctance, and immediately intervened, Now then, what do we have here? An actor with stage-fright? And he laughed a raucous weaselly laugh, Perhaps it's you that should play that stupid faithful Duke, he growled at me and spat in my face as he did so. Perhaps you're the one that needs to be blinded, and he raised his whip towards my cheek preparing to place his strike. Before I could tell him that that indeed was what I felt, Carl had turned his back on us and was already entering into his fate as Gloucester, by dragging one of the benches across and pretending to no longer hear what the guard was saying. Nor did he appear to take notice of what was happening behind him. Instead, like a revered director and with an all-commanding body language, he conveyed to us that he – a master of space and timing – was in complete control of the acting area and that the performance was now to begin.

Here, grab this bench, he called to me in a gruff and irritated voice, as he suddenly got between me and the guard. No, not like that, stupid, it needs to be placed like this, you idiot, Carl grunted, as I was about to let it drop to the ground too soon and position it in a different way.

This was to be the bench upon which Carl was to be strapped.

Was he trying to make me hate him.Was he trying to make my job easier? It was hard for me to tell. Carl was so convincing, even now. He had suddenly changed completely and it was as if a block of frozen air had wedged itself between us.

As the guard settled down to watch the spectacle, he tossed a piece of flint towards me. We knew of the beatings of prisoners by prisoners. For the fun of the guards. We, too had experienced it several times since our arrival here. And in such situations prisoners would try, if possible, to play-act, to feign pain and scream out if necessary to make it appear as though they'd been truly wounded, even before they had been. Carl had also spent many hours rehearsing fighting scenes with the youngsters so that they could master this vital skill, this survival skill. But this was different. This was for real. And my mind instinctively returned to the tiger on the Steppes. I stiffened every sinew in my body, widened and extended my eyes, and forced them to be like a blank mirror as I tried desperately to disengage my emotions.

Much about what happened next, I no longer recall. I remember blood streaming down Carl's cheeks, I remember Carl remaining quite still and not struggling too much. I remember silence.

Strange though it may seem, I don't remember hearing any sound from him. It was as if Carl had steeled himself to his fate and chosen the attitude he was going to adopt. That was his last thread of freedom which he still retained, which he still clung on to.

I would later learn from Lena that Carl had silently repeated Lear's lines to himself throughout the ordeal, It will come, humanity must perforce prey on itself like monsters of the deep. Like monsters of the deep. Monsters of the deep. That's what he'd kept repeating to himself. These words had become his mantra. Humanity was a word and concept which our oppressors hated. Carl believed in a humanity which would not be forever suppressed and forever prey to each other. That's why he'd uttered these lines, I remember thinking as Lena told me about Carl's thoughts many years later. By uttering this absolute pessimism in his bleakest hour, it strengthened his inner resolve and gave him the will to fight against man's inhumanity to man. By uttering these lines, he was in fact fighting against them. That had always been his life-saving strategy. That's what had given him strength, that's what gave him the necessary energy and somehow allowed him to rise above my actions. Until he finally lost consciousness.

The guard's fun with us quickly evaporated as soon as he saw the lorries appearing on the horizon. He jumped to his feet, straightened his jacket which still bore the letter J roughly stitched to the back, shouted at his workers to get ready and rushed towards his post. He knew his life would also be in jeopardy from his overseers if he were found to be neglecting his duties.

A young man hurried past the bench on which Carl was still strapped and threw me a torn-off strip of cloth from his jacket. I hastened to tie it round Carl's head. Then I kissed him quickly before joining the rest of the inmates now all lined up on one side of the quarry and with pick-axes in their hands.

That day it was as if nature were also working against us, as if nature were also conspiring against the most vulnerable, as torrents of icy rain poured from the Heavens. Yet we were not allowed to stop working. We still had our daily quota to fulfil and had to work twice as hard due to the lateness of the lorries. And all the while Carl lay completely abandoned to his fate. Unattended. Whilst puddles of red water gradually accumulated by the legs of the bench. Every now and then, and when the guard wasn't looking, I glanced over to where Carl lay motionless.

Yet I didn't look at Carl. Not at his face. Not at his wound. Instead, I looked at the puddles. I studied them. I became transfixed by the patterns that were gradually forming, the shapes that were being made in the chalky gravelly ground. The shapes that then dissipated as big hail stones hit them and bounced back up in the air again. The kaleidoscopic patterns of red on greyish-white clods of chalk distracted me from my act and transported me into a different world. I continued to watch as bubbles formed in the puddles once the hailstones had ceased and given way to rain. I watched as they bobbed around on the surface for a while, before they merged with others to form one big bubble which continued to float for a while until it suddenly burst. As if pricked by a tiny pin.

When the labour shift finally came to an end, it had seemed like the longest day I had ever worked. Time had stood still for the most part, and I, too, had entered a different state of consciousness. It was the other fellows with whom I was working that had managed to bring me back to some kind of reality. But it was to the grim reality of Carl's horrific fate that I returned, when we were eventually allowed to unstrap him from the bench. We struggled to bundle Carl into our jackets which we had knotted together to form a stretcher of sorts, and then we carried him back to our base, cradled like a baby, whilst we stumbled constantly under the dead weight.

~ ~ ~

All was not lost, however, for Carl. Amazingly, that evening, we found a bed for him in one of the barracks for the sick. We had to leave him at the entrance and were not permitted to accompany him inside. It was, however, Carl's great fortune at his darkest moment of despair that Lena had been assigned to work nearby and that she would soon learn of his fate and seek him out. That much I knew. Yet, she never would know what had really happened that day in the quarry. She never would know that I was the one who had betrayed Carl. During all the hours that Lena nursed Carl, he never told her how his eyesight had been lost. Perhaps he had managed to erase the act. But it would be my inescapable fate to keep it alive. To keep seeing it in my mind. To keep feeling it in my heart.

Hey, come on, Lena, Carl joked some time after he'd regained consciousness, and once his wounds had begun to congeal and he'd had a few days of food and drink inside him, No one can take away the light I have inside me, you know that. It may not be as bright now, he playfully added, but it's still there. I still shine. I still burn, oh how I still burn! he quipped flirtatiously, and groped his way towards her, hoping to find her hand or arm near his.

Lena was perched on the edge of the bed, she later told me. He knew her scent, he could measure and size up her presence, and his whole body cried out to her through the searing pain. See, how you feel me burn, he insisted, as he tried to suppress the stabbing pain, eventually found her hand, and made his way up her forearm, her elbow and then to her shoulder which he gently squeezed. You feel it, I know you do, I know you do, I burn with love, ah, my Lena, how I burn, burn, he had quipped, although rather feebly.

As Carl's voice gradually faded, his fingers slowly slipped from Lena's shoulder to the subtle incline of her breast and along to the upturn of her pert nipple. His thumb lay there for a few moments, as if suspended as it rested lightly above the swelling, the softly beating swelling of her tiny breast. His fingers hung limply for some moments, before carefully cupping themselves around the underside of her breast and gathering it up ever so gently as they did so. He then held it quite still from beneath. The heat of his fingers slowly penetrated it as he began to push lightly against the sides with his palms, until he held the weight completely in his hand again.

After some time, he released his hold and let his fingers brush round her breast like a feather lightly caressing it before letting them descend in a spiralling motion into her lap. And there his hand rested again. In the warmth of Lena's lap. After a while, he slowly slipped his hand between her legs, and his fingers settled once more without moving. They just rested, until at last Carl could feel her moistness beneath the coarseness of her garments.

He began to press his fingers and thumb against her, lightly and rhythmically, then, with ever so slightly increasing pressure, as he tried desperately to counteract the pain gripping his whole body. It was a pain which now mingled desire, love and hurt. They were still the only parts of their bodies that were touching, that were yielding, and the rough cloth still lay between them. There was no rush, there were no hurried movements. The night was theirs. That is how Lena had later recounted this moment. She must have wanted to convey to me Carl's tenderness.

~ ~ ~

Lena had a plan. Perhaps she'd already told Carl about it during their last night together. Or perhaps their last night together had been the trigger for her plan.

I later learned that Lena had been a peripheral member of the group that had helped to sabotage one of the gas chambers in the final months before liberation. Miraculously, she had not been caught. Her involvement with the sabotage had not been suspected. Her secret messages had not been found and the women who were caught did not betray her. She'd passed her messages to one of them working alongside a civilian worker who had connections to the partisan group outside the camp. This person had then transmitted them on to one of the resistance inmates working in the munitions factory. Most would be unaware of Lena's identity or of the fact that her messages had helped to organise the clandestine operation even though she herself could not gain access to the grenades.

Lena's own plan was to effect an escape and to take some of the youngsters with her, the ones who would be more likely to survive the tough ordeal of walking for miles without water, food or shelter and taking refuge in dugouts before the safe house some seven kilometres away could be reached. But Lena also bided her time. She gave little value to her present predicament, although the conditions in the camp were becoming dire as the administrative and organisational structures began to crumble. The guards were also becoming more agitated and unpredictable than usual. The golden rules Lena had learnt early on in her confinement became more relevant than ever, always act as though you are following all the orders…but do everything possible to sabotage and deceive the oppressors and protect the inmates. Always behave as if you are more stupid than the oppressors, they are more primitive than the most primitive.

To the world controlled by her guards, Lena continued to do her duties and work, hastening to obey every absurd new rule and regulation that came her way. But she had also managed to link up with the resistance organisation within the camp. Her work in the hospital enabled her to smuggle out medicines, negatives of photographs taken inside the camp and at the crematoria, illegal literature, and lists of those who had been shot or gassed.

She filled her thoughts with freedom and waited for the right moment. She waited for the right moment to execute her own escape plan which had already been secretly communicated to those immediately outside the camp, and who had arranged assistance for her both within and outside the camp when the moment arrived.

That moment did not come until early December. She wasn't just waiting though. She was strengthening her resolve and her determination to survive and to save at least a few lives, if possible. And she thought about what Carl had once told her about the Renaissance artists – about their mental and physical preparations before they began work on painting the cupola of a church and how they had deliberately deprived themselves of certain bodily pleasures. How they had found it essential to stop eating meat three months before starting the work, to stop drinking wine two months before and to refrain from sexual activities one month before. He told her how they had then placed an arm in plaster and the day that they were to begin their work, they would break the plaster and take a brush and paint a perfect circle.

She thought about Tibetan monks who were able to produce an inner heat by visualising the cells in their bodies and meditating upon the huge amount of energy lying dormant within each cell and how they were able to increase this energy by repeating certain mantras.

And she remembered Carl as he lay in his make-shift hospital bed. She remembered how he had continued to stare upwards even then, with his bandaged eyes, and just as he had always done whilst lying on the plank-bed of the previous place, When I stare at these planks above me, she remembered him telling her during their last night, I see a pool of water, dappled with sunlight and caressed by the trailing branches of surrounding trees as they sway gently in the currents of air. Threads of spiders' webs, glistening silver and gold, hang delicately down from the branches. And just above the shimmering water, I watch tiny summer gnats dancing in circles of perpetual motion. Up and down, round and round. I watch and I feel as light as a feather. And in the pool I gaze at the patterns of light which slowly fluctuate in shape with the softly swirling waters and with the shifting shadows of the trees and leaves. And as I peer deeper into the pool, into its darkness with sparkling specks of refracted sunlight, it is as if I have seen and drunk of the whole Universe. And it is at such moments that I know that life will always flow and will never stay still. And no photograph and no image can replace this fluid and ephemeral moment of oneness.

It was in December when some of the last trains were transporting inmates away from the camp and from the advancing armies that Lena seized her chance to escape with a small group of children into the surrounding woodlands. It was a miraculous escape and Lena was certainly lucky. But she needed more than luck. Her earlier work with resistance groups and her local knowledge had proven vital to her and her group's survival. She had also rehearsed the plan with her contact person for several weeks beforehand and this person had also procured the necessary equipment, documents and civilian clothing which they needed for their escape, and had placed them in the agreed spot hidden beneath one of the empty barracks, and ready for Lena and her group to retrieve at the arranged time on the arranged day. Lena had been more fortunate than others who had attempted to escape this way some months before – many of whom had been rounded up in the houses or roads nearby, or who had been shot before even reaching the camp's perimeter. Despite the subsequent torture of the surviving escapees, they had not divulged the hide-out and the mechanics of the escape.

Before too long, and with the help of a couple of civilian workers, Lena had managed to link up with partisan groups first outside the camp, and then not far from the main town some thirty miles away. And it was the partisan group which had been able to secure them a safe house in one of the coalmining towns nearby, and where they would then hide until the liberators arrived.

Lena managed to save three lives. Three young lives who would recount their adventurous escape for years to come. The escape and the minute details of it provided them with a means of shielding themselves from the horrors that preceded it. It was the escape that they kept reliving in their minds. It was the escape which would be the focus and memory of their time in Hell.

Carl had been right. He knew I'd not be able just to get on with life once the camp had been liberated. Most of all, I needed to avenge his death. His death that symbolised so many deaths. So much suffering. Perhaps most of all, I had to free myself of my own complicity in the horrors. And the only way I could see to do that was to take the whole misery out on the one person whom I could most clearly identify as the cause of my suffering. The one I saw as having compromised my humanity, and who'd made me into the monster I still saw myself to be. It was the guard who had made of me a predator of the one I loved most in life. It was he who took my soul. That's what I believed over the years.

Revenge, however, came dripping slow. I was the patient one. I could take my time and choose the right moment once I'd hunted down my victim. Once I'd sniffed him out. It was many years, however, before I picked up his scent. But once I had, I followed him for months and marked out his territory, watched his every move and until I could predict his movements almost instinctively.

It was at a celebratory banquet that I chose my moment. He was waving a glass of red wine in the air and was about to make a toast. He was quite a famous actor now. Carl would have appreciated life's ironies, I remember thinking when I discovered this. He was toasting a whole host of people who had come together to fête the final performance of the Shakespeare season. Another of life's ironies.

He no longer knew me, that much I could tell, as I slowly made my way to where he was standing. I smiled at him as I approached him. He responded with a slightly puzzled look on his face. I greeted him with my eyes as I came face to face with him, quietly reassuring him with another smile. I then removed the glass from his outstretched hand and gently tipped it over his head. In one slow but deliberate movement. I watched as the red wine sluggishly trickled round his eyes, and then slipped along the creases of his skin. It was as if time were suspended. I watched as the dark red liquid gradually and jerkily wound its way to his crisp-white shirt.

He now knew. He now knew who I was, yet he did not utter a word. He knew his guilt, even though he had tried to bury it. He, too, had carried it deep within him for many years. Then I saw his eyes fill with fear as I whipped out my pocket-knife from my jacket. A glint from the poison-tipped blade flashed at him as I flicked it open. I held it firmly in my hand. And with one lunging movement I slit his throat from left to right, the poison ensuring him an even quicker death. In the wake of this ritualistic blood-letting I suddenly and instinctively released a long pent-up primeval cry. And for one brief moment I finally had control of my life again.

Except I didn't. It was that moment of revenge, that blind act of revenge, which cast me into an even greater Hell. It was the Hell of my own mind and the horrors within. The horrors created by what I'd witnessed during those nightmarish years. The horrors which now crashed in on me in one huge mass and left me completely stranded. Stranded and suspended in a state of madness from which it would take me years to break free. Years of Hell on Earth. Years of darkness. Years of every imaginable misery known to man. Years of feeling everything I knew, everything I had witnessed, everything that had been done and that I had also done, and then magnified millions of times.

~ ~ ~

Now you're mine, you're truly mine, you've done your time, your time for your crime, a year that's all, mercy was great, justice more thrifty, but now we'll wander together, wander through this mystery, and you'll feel time and space, altogether differently. This was how the voice, which would accompany me through my years of darkness, first introduced itself to me on my release from prison. With each utterance the voice drew nearer until I could just about make out the irregular shape of a darkly cloaked creature. Yet I couldn't trace whether it was man or beast. It seemed to be able to hover, walk and also crawl very close to the ground as it approached me. But before I could perceive any of its features, it suddenly leapt into the air and attached itself to my back whilst its claw-like wings clamped themselves around my neck. And there it hung, not moving, not making any more sounds for quite some time. I, too, did not move, could not move. It was as if I had become petrified by this creature. It was as if this creature had taken sole charge of my movements and of my thoughts.

It was then that a shrieking and howling noise began to pierce through me. I couldn't escape it. I tried pressing my hands firmly against my ears whilst I held my eyes tightly shut, yet the noise would not cease. I could feel the beating of my eardrums within, I could feel the beating getting louder and more forceful as I tried to suppress the shrieking and howling.

The Bearer of Darkness now has you at last, it suddenly began to chant, once the noise had become fainter and more disjointed, To test and torment you, to work through the past. And then it squealed a long shriek of menacing delight. I turned my head first left and then right, straining to see as far behind me as possible, but it was as if it could anticipate my every move and was always one step ahead of me. I could hear it, I could feel it, yet I couldn't see it well enough to define it.

I'm the vulture, the raven, the man-bird of yore, I'm drawn to my prey, by its own vengeful call, continued the voice, before erupting into another piercing shriek, and then resuming in a rather indifferent yet weary voice, Come let us not tarry, we've so much to see, we've crimes to avenge, we've corpses to free. And suddenly I felt its claw-like wings clinging to my eyelids and lashes. And as it hung there, it created a stabbing-like sensation that darted from my lids and through my eyeballs before lodging into the back of my head like thousands of embedded knives.

With a fierce jerk I felt the creature move in front of me to pull us both away. As it turned round to look at me, I found not a face but a never-ending blackness. A blackness into which its shape dissolved. And as I was moved to follow it, it felt as though I, too, was dissolving into an ever-increasing black hole.

These deeds that haunt you so, their source lies in the past, it's the past to where we'll go, so hold on tight. And the voice screeched another shriek as we were sucked upwards into an even bigger black hole on a descending then ascending flash of light. With each electric surge my whole body convulsed as we rode on flashes of lightning that cracked and crackled. And as the lightning changed direction, we were tossed this way and that, and my head was whipped backwards by the jolts. And with each flash, the darkness revealed distorted and mutilated faces, first only a few, and then hundreds and thousands of them, and they stared at me from behind their rigid death masks. They stared and stared, then crowded in on me, and bore right through to my marrow. I couldn't hide, I couldn't retreat, and when I tried to close my eyes the faces were still with me. And I could do nothing for them, yet still they stared.

Then suddenly the lightning ceased and everything turned black.

Yet I still hung suspended in the darkness, with the creature wrapped tightly around my head and body. An eerie silence and heavy atmosphere enveloped me. It felt as though I were suffocating. And just as my eyes were about to close and finally find rest, they were wrenched open once more by the claw-like wings of my keeper, as it began to screech and howl in a feverishly high pitch, before declaring, The faces you saw, are mine now to keep, their crime was to live, live at the wrong time, we'll now let them sleep. Then it pierced the air with another of its screeches, And now onwards we'll tread, there's lots more to see, we've the killers yet to find, the souls still to free, from the evil monster's heads.

Then in a slow deliberate movement, I was dragged sideways by the man-bird, as it began to haul me past rows and rows of lined-up faces. All grey, all completely expressionless. But all different in features and form. The creature clamped its claws round the sides of my head as if to force me to look at each face, to stare into each pair of eyes which stared back at me, which stared back at me blankly. Soullessly.

I seemed to look into hundreds and thousands of faces as we moved along in painfully slow motion. I looked, I stared and I found nothing. I found nothing until eventually I came face to face with my own. Blank. Soulless. No spark of life. But not because I was numbed to my own crime, but because it had completely taken over me.

We stood still and as I became more and more transfixed, the creature loosened its grip. And as I continued to look into my own eyes, I saw them begin to soften round the edges and I saw colour begin to emerge in the iris. I watched as lightly etched lines formed in the skin around the corners of my eyes. I watched as they slowly turned towards the left, to where I could just about make out another face. A man's face. His eyes slowly greeted mine, as I caught sight of him, although I still couldn't quite assemble his features into a complete image. His eyes pierced the darkness. Strikingly so. Then they began to smile at me. Until they almost disappeared, as a broad grin erupted across his face. It was then that I heard that chuckle. That old familiar chuckle.

After what seemed like minutes, everything turned yellow and I felt a warm calmness spread through my veins and caress my body from the inside out. Then with a sudden bump, I felt myself drop onto solid ground, and my eyes flew wide open with the jolt.

It was twenty four years later. And beside me I found Lena, and Lena was dabbing the sweat from my cheek. She was talking about Carl. She was talking about Carl and about our special friendship.

~ ~ ~

Why have I told you all this, you are probably asking yourselves? Why now, why here, why in this way? I paused and scanned the faces of the academics, the scientists, the scholars. I had learnt much from Carl. I had learnt to anticipate, measure and fill time in a way which allowed for an interaction with 'the other', also for an invisible or inaudible interaction. Energy, the energy from words and actions, moved in mysterious ways. Mysterious because energy is all too often completely invisible to most of us, most of the time. I remember Carl having told his youngsters this one day. We can never really know how our words, actions and silences will be received by others, but we have bestowed upon us the reasoning and intellect to strive to achieve a greater good for all, regardless of nationality, race, creed, species. His years of confinement had taught him that. He hadn't just guided the youngsters in their acting, he'd also tried to guide them in their preparation for a meaningful life.

Shakespeare knew that life is fragile and that it could be ended all too easily with a little pin. Carl hadn't shied away from conveying this to his youngsters, I told my audience. But he had shielded them from the horrors of torture. He did not want them to envisage what it was like to become completely of flesh and to be made into a prey of death whilst still clinging to life.

The audience was mostly German. And they were mostly quite young. They had come to hear me speak about Carl, and about Carl's last years. Yet, I had needed to tell them more. I'd needed to tell them about revenge, and why Carl had not really felt it, but I had. I'd needed to tell them of my actions and of my years of darkness.

Yet, I'd also wanted to tell them about the role of academics in the persecution, deportation and killing, about how they had fuelled the fire of hatred and contempt and had legitimised it with their many publications. How they had scorned and taunted Germany with their comparisons of its people to a Hamlet who fails to act until it is too late and is torn apart by indecision. How, when Germany got its man of action, they had done little or nothing to question or criticise the acts which were then unleashed.

And then there were the countless publications which used science for political ends to assert and justify racial superiority and proclaim the inferiority of others. There were also the academic institutes which were set up and lavishly funded to map out vast geographical and population areas in a way that would later facilitate the oppressors' plans for deportations, repatriations and mass murder. And there were the institutes that were funded for their medical experiments for the perfect race.

Academics had helped pave the way for people to be led into blind indiscriminate actions, and to a horrific destruction of so-called undesirables. They had eagerly worked on ways of promoting a perfect race. But it was the connivance of lawyers and judges that had legitimised and put into practice the whole process of terror, torture and destruction. Shamelessly so. By increment. From beginning to end. And most had continued in their professions even after this was known. Seamlessly so. Little detriment had they suffered, and many were promoted or even commended and honoured.

My guard was small fry. He was largely the victim of his own inadequacies and sadistic mind, whilst the power-hugging and hat-doffing suited men who had manufactured and executed that world of fear, hatred and destruction, had mostly been absolved of complicity, of the brutality of their unquestioning actions. They were the slippery ones – the ones who were least easy to catch and pin down, the ones that had also felt little guilt about their actions and thoughts.

I'd wanted to tell the audience all this because I didn't want it to happen again. To anyone. Anywhere. I didn't want the youngsters to witness or be part of what had been thrust upon us. I wanted them to see the warning signs, to sniff the air like the gazelle on the Plains, and to know when an ill wind is blowing. And I wanted them to know how to stand their ground in the face of adversity or danger. To know how to keep in focus their wild and untamed side. To guard it with their life. To remember that they could still discover it, even when downtrodden. I wanted to tell them that it was their wild streak which could give them the strength and the courage to withstand or confront oppression, but also to escape. Just as I had told Carl all those years ago when I first arrived at the camp. But I also didn't want them to take revenge. Not to act out of revenge. That is not what I now understood about taking a stand. And it was Carl who had tried to tell me this. It was Carl who'd tried to warn me against it.

Carl's dream didn't end with the multi-headed monster. Years later Lena told me about a dream Carl had had the night before he perished. The dream began as the others had with Carl lying in a pasture of yellow flowers. The dream quickly propelled Carl once more into the depths of the seas, through the cavernous trench and down to the underwater flame-stoked graveyard. Only this time, the lashing tongues of fire had turned into a bubbling roaring inferno, and hot molten rocks were spewing up all around it.

Carl managed to find the bones of the children once again. But the bones were not as before. Something was different. Instead of being surrounded by creeping tendrils and slimy bladderwrack, this time he saw tresses of hair emerging from beneath them. Then the hair began to float and swirl in the raging waters which were still spinning all around them.

As Carl peered more intensely into the murkiness of the graveyard, the darkness gradually became studded with beads of many colours and dotted with a myriad of patterns made out of pearls. Eventually he could perceive the orbs of thousands of pairs of eyes. And as he continued to stare, the bones became clothed once more in flesh, at first bruised, torn and breached by wounds, but then peach-like in texture and colour. And the children slowly began to rise from their rotten cradle of mud. And as they rose they began to shake the monster's tentacles which were still holding them captive, first hesitatingly and then more vigorously. As more children began to reappear, the monster's heads also multiplied. His swollen heads were as hungry as ever. The situation was still desperate and I was still trying to chop off its heads.

A few children caught sight of Carl and began to scream out their names to him, screaming as loudly as they could above the inferno. More joined in. Soon tens of names penetrated his ears, then hundreds upon hundreds, until they merged into an eerie discordant chorus which became more and more insistent and shrill. Just at the point where Carl felt that he could no longer bear it, the strange fish appeared once more.

They had a new message for him. Carl had to release the children. Not by slaying the monster's many heads. All that had proven futile. The children could only be freed by the calling out of their names. By remembering every single one. By forgetting no one.

And do you know what, my friend, Lena had proudly announced, as I awoke from my years

of darkness, and as I awoke to her calling me in the same way as Carl had always done, He told me that he remembered them all. Every one of them. And as she said this, she let out a hearty laugh, He had even amazed himself in this dream, she continued, As he began to call the first few names, his voice gradually broke into a mellifluous invocation which flowed and flowed. And with the rhythmic chant the violently swirling water began to grow calmer and settled into gentle undulating rhythms. And with the calmness, light suddenly became visible in the depths. The children also began to join in with the chanting. Soon golden threads were weaving their way through the waters linking the children to one another and eventually a thread also reached Carl. But before it reached Carl, Carl suddenly called my name, and the name of our child that had not yet been born. I was cradling the child in the furthest corner of the graveyard. On hearing my name, I looked up and smiled across at Carl. And as a golden thread attached itself to me, we all floated upwards together and towards the opening breast of the sea, now rose-flushed with the dawn of a new day. And just at the point where air meets water, Carl laughed. And as Carl laughed, I kissed the sun-soaked primeval breast of Mother Nature.
We were free…

What Lena was unable to tell me that day, was that the day after this dream Carl had entered the chamber of death.

But I knew from what Lena had just recounted to me that his mind had already been in a different place when he entered that final man-made chamber of Hell. He'd already created a perfect end. He'd cheated his oppressors. In his own way.

And so, my friends, I want to close my talk with a few lines from a poet, whose work I have come to admire. I think Carl would have liked these lines. And these lines remind me of Carl and of Carl's dream,

We die with the dying
See, they depart, and we go with them.
We are born with the dead
See, they return, and bring us with them.

I turned towards Carl and gestured to be led. Carl, Lena's and Carl's son, was now my eyes as he helped me out of the hall and into the cool night air. As the air gently caressed my sunken lips, I sensed that I, too, was free.

AFTERWORD

Conference presentation given by the author at Aberystwyth, Wales and Naples, Italy (see 'Lo Straniero', no. 36) in 2002

Staged Communication: Theresienstadt. A Tragedy in 6 Acts and a Warning for the future

'Staged communication' is the term I use to refer to authorised and non-authorised communication which is staged; that is to say performed on stage or the equivalent and for an audience. It also encompasses communication which is stage-managed, that is to say carefully orchestrated and controlled for effect which may be for constructive or pernicious ends. It is the destructive side of such 'staged communication' which I wish to focus on here as witnessed by the developments with and within Theresienstadt.
Theresienstadt is symbolic of the role of deception as a powerful and lethal weapon in diplomacy and policy. It is also a tragedy in six acts, and at the same time a warning for the way contemporary political issues are perhaps being 'staged' in such a way, that 'crimes' against people may once again be hidden.

Prologue

1941. At the very heart of Europe in the middle of Bohemia, lies a small garrison town called Theresienstadt (an hour north of Prague) which is about to play a central role in deception on a massive scale. Bismarck once said: '*He who controls Bohemia, also controls Europe*'. In Oct 1941 Theresienstadt is first mentioned in connection with the Nazi's plans for the Final Solution; a few months later at the Wannsee conference it is referred to as a ghetto for the old and privileged. The illusion the Nazis wish to present to the outside world is of Theresienstadt as a model spa town and old people's holiday camp with leisure opportunities for all to enjoy – a deception which would later be underpinned by a film with the unofficial title: 'Der Führer schenkt den Juden eine Stadt (The Führer gives the Jews a town).' The drawings, writings and songs created clandestinely by inmates within Theresienstadt, and which to some extent have survived, present an altogether different picture.

This small town of Theresienstadt is suddenly targeted by the SS because they needed an alibi to divert attention from the radical nature of deportations and the extermination programme; the SS also needed to solve the world's interest in and concern for endangered prominent personalities; and last, but by no means least, the SS needed a ruse to confiscate as much wealth and capital in the process.

Act One Setting up the Illusion

The illusion was set up basically using normal bureaucratic procedures and Nazi communication structures already in place under the Reich. For the German and Austrian Jews, the first they heard of it was a misleading advert in newspapers which promised an idyllic place to spend your retirement, in exchange for surrendering, for instance, your valuables, savings, home. The illusion was made all the more credible with the *Heimeinkaufvertrag* – the contract which guaranteed a place in the home and often with a room of your choice. Behind the scenes and at the *Reichssicherheitsamt* (main security office and Gestapo levels) Theresienstadt was known all along as a *Lager*, and, within the bureaucratic system from early 1942 onwards, as *Altersghetto bzw. Durchgangslager nach Auschwitz* (old people's home, that is to say transit camp to Auschwitz). Thus, Theresienstadt was never intended as the end-destination for the Jews, and yet they were led to believe this would be the case.

The deception was accompanied by blackmail. The Jews were ordered to sign a declaration of their assets – a *Vermögenserklärung,* and a willingness to surrender them in exchange for a place in this home. A few months later this illusion was no longer needed, as they were declared to be *volks- und staatsfeindlich* (enemies of the people and state). Thus, they automatically lost their citizenship which enabled the SS (in collusion with the bureaucratic, legal and financial apparatus) to confiscate assets.
Promises were made to the first Jewish leader, Jakob Edelstein, that he would be able to set up a Jewish community with its own autonomy and with its self-governing council of Elders. Thus, rumours spread that Theresienstadt was also a Jewish community and not just a retirement home. In reality the Nazis had organised it as a camp with a *Lagerkommandant* (camp commander), an SS-officer who gave orders to the leader of Jews.
The Jews were also led to believe that they would be travelling to this Spa-town as normal citizens. Thus, they paid for the transport to Theresienstadt themselves and were booked on as normal passengers in proper trains. Yet, cattle trucks were then used for the most part.
The fact that everything had to be executed in a correct manner and in a clinical way, meant that many parties would not, at first, have been aware of the true nature of the plan. The re-settlement to Theresienstadt was indeed legitimately processed, and assisted by the forced collusion of the *Reichsvereinigung der Juden in Deutschland.* Thus, this contributed to the great deception and the great success with which the high-ranking SS and Gestapo were able to execute the final solution plan without too much meddling from others.

Act Two *Confronting the Reality behind the Illusion: Survial Strategies*

Theresientstadt was no spa-town, nor self-governing ghetto. Nor would it be allowed to develop in such directions. As soon as the first German-Austrian Jews arrived, they were confronted with a heavily guarded camp and, within this, a council of Jewish leaders who were answerable to the SS-commander. The SS-commander gave the instructions and the leaders had to set about organising the logistics. Such instructions included the selection of thousands of Jews for transports to the East.

The first few months were mainly spent settling in and setting up a microcosm of society. In reality this actually involved the setting up of sanitary systems, electricity supplies and building bakeries in order to cater for a population expansion in the town from 7000 to 50 000 in a matter of a couple of months. Alongside these essential practicalities, cultural activities were encouraged as a way of helping the people deal with their emotions, including the traumatic shock of realising the true status of Theresienstadt with its hunger, disease, misery and high death rate. Such cultural activities included theatrical productions, classical concerts, lectures and even cabaret, and all performances were soon booked out. The fact that many European artists were sent to Theresienstadt in the first instance meant that such events were often of high quality.

The leaders of the Jews encouraged their people to build this community 'as if': 'As if' it truly were a viable prospect as a strategy for coping with the present. On a practical level all kinds of euphemisms were used to support a positive state of mind – thus, dry bread was referred to as 'toast'; hunger as 'vitamin deficiency'. Such deliberate self-deception was often made fun of in the cabarets. Indeed, with the desire for escapism being so great, some inmates began to believe in the power of the leaders, and believed that Theresienstadt was, or at least could become, an autonomous community. The unforeseen danger for some was that self-deception no longer became a survival strategy, but a permanent state of mind.

The first internal and external conflicts were brought to a head with the onset of transports to the East in the autumn of 1942. The Jewish leaders not only had to deal yet again with the double-dealing by the SS, they were then faced with the impossible choice of selecting the people for the transports East for the numbers stated by the SS.

This practice often fostered jealousy, envy and fear, and brought out the worst characteristics in people. Lying became a legitimate practice.

In an extreme effort to retain their sense of dignity, civilisation and community, the Jews were unwittingly playing into the hands of the Nazis. By taking their duties so seriously, which included drawing up contracts for actors and performers and procedures for rehearsals, they legitimized the present, the awful deception, rather than negating it (H.G. Adler).

In so doing, the constructive and destructive forces which were at play came into tragic conflict with one another as the inmates tried to control the environment. This is the classic material for tragedy: the very activity of the conscious will, seeking a way out, unwittingly helped to create the conditions which precipitated the mass-deception: had the inmates realised the true evil intent of the Nazis, they would perhaps have reacted to the situation in a different way. The tragic climax unfolded proper in the summer of 1944.

Act Three *Staging the Illusion*

From December 1943 until June 1944 Theresienstadt was gradually transformed into a stage set for the purposes of deceiving the outside world. The Jewish inmates were now forced to create a façade of what the SS were purporting Theresienstadt to be in the original advertisements.

The inmates were not told the purpose of the embellishment plan and hopes were raised. In actual fact, the inmates were effectively turned into stage-hands and stage-designers, preparing the scenery and settings for a visit by the International Red Cross. The audience, the Red Cross, had been requesting this visit for two years. In June 1943 reports in the press were already referring to Theresienstadt as an alibi for the extermination programme.

Not only was Theresienstadt turned into a massive stage-set for six hours (the duration of the International Red Cross visit), with pretend banks, shops, cafés and schools and with ornamental parks and play areas, it became a play within a play, a theatre-show within the theatre of Theresienstadt, and within the theatre of the war and extermination policies in general. The actors, the inmates, were nearly 60,000 in number.

The performance space, the town of Theresienstadt, took nearly seven months to prepare. The script was also carefully orchestrated and controlled. Rehearsals were ordered of certain artistic works, and yet the inmates remained oblivious as to the reason for the cosmetic illusion and preparations, nor did they know who the potential audience would be.

The day of 23 June 1944 arrived and the three Red Cross delegates (accompanied throughout by the SS and the camp commander) were introduced to a few key people and watched, amongst other things, carefully staged performances of jazz music by the 'Ghetto-swingers' and of the children's opera 'Brundibar', and of Kurt Gerron's cabaret 'Karrusell'. The delegates mainly based their reports on second-hand information from the SS and from Eppstein (the Jewish leader since 1943). The propaganda triumphed, the 'staged communication' achieved its intended effect. The

Red Cross just saw what they were shown, they only saw what they were supposed to. They did not see the hunger, the misery, the overcrowding, the slave work, the diseases and high death rate, and most importantly, they did not see the transports leaving for the East.
The Swiss delegate, Dr Rossel, wrote in his summary: '*Wir werden sagen, daß unser Erstaunen außerordentlich war, im Ghetto eine Stadt zu finden, die fast ein normales Leben lebt...Diese jüdische Stadt ist tatsächlich erstaunlich...Das Ghetto von Theresienstadt ist eine kommunistische Gesellschaft, die von einem 'Stalin' von hohem Wert geleitet wird.*'
(We will say that we were greatly astounded to find a town in the ghetto which was almost leading a normal life...this Jewish town is truly amazing...the ghetto of Theresienstadt is a communist society which is governed by a 'Stalin' of high standing).

Act Four Filming the Staged Illusion

The greatest feat of deception and the climax of the tragedy is the 'Jewish-produced' film of the illusion. The idea for this seems to have stemmed from SS Sturmführer/major Günther around December 1943. Although the film did not go through the propaganda channels, Himmler could also have known of it, without authorising it. Some initial filming began in January 1944 with the Czech Jindrich Weil, but it was not until March 1945 that it was complete with final edits. The official title of the film: 'Theresienstadt. Ein Dokumentarfilm aus dem jüdischen Siedlungsgebiet' was supposed to lend an aura of objectivity to the film.
The main part of the filming lasted eleven days from 16 August to 11 September 1944. During this time the inmates of Theresienstadt became film actors and the SS and the guards became editors and producers. Theresienstadt effectively became 'the Hollywood of the concentration

camps' (see H.G. Adler 1958 for comprehensive documentation on Theresienstadt). Whereas some inmates lost themselves completely in the illusion and thoroughly entered into the spirit of the propaganda, others had to be forced via blackmail or duress into taking part. Others saw through the absurdity of this ghostly satire and poked fun at it with cleverly worded letters to the producers.
Kurt Gerron, the famous Berlin actor, had a major role in directing the film, whilst Jo Spiers drew hundreds of small sketches. These sketches are an invaluable testimony to the making of the film. The sketches were not a story-board for the filming, but rather depict the images Spiers saw through the camera lens in the course of the filming.
The film not only masks reality and conceals the Jews' own holocaust, the Jews also appear to have financed it. The funds for the film (35 000RM) were met by the Zentralstelle's financial resources which consisted of confiscated Jewish capital.

Act Five Selling the Illusion: Editing in the Desired Effect

The film was intended for a foreign audience, as a way of appeasing growing concerns and fears for the safety of Jews. It was edited, not following Gerron's suggestions, but instead, relied on the Prague editor Fric (closely supervised by the SS) who prepared *Aktualita*'s weekly news sreenings for the SS. At one point, the film depicts Jews relaxing in a café, then there is an immediate cut to the scene of fighting soldiers with noises of bomb explosions in the background. The suggestive message is then emphasised by a voice-over: '*Während in Theresienstadt Juden bei Kaffee und Kuchen sitzen und tanzen, tragen unsere Soldaten alle Lasten eines furchtbaren Krieges, Not und Entbehrungen, um die Heimat zu verteidigen*' (Whilst the Jews enjoy coffee and cake and dance, our soldiers are

bearing all the weight of a terrible war, necessity and hardships, in order to defend our country).
There were four documented screenings of the film. One in Prague for the State-minister Frank and high-ranking SS, and three screenings in Theresienstadt for foreign organisations including the International Red Cross (16 April 1945) and representatives from the Hungarian-Jewish Rescue Committee (later on 16 April 1945), at which Eichmann himself was present.
These represent Eichmann's final attempts to exploit the fraud of the model ghetto.
The emotional impact of the film and its narrated myth was so great that the deception still continues. The Jews, in bitter recognition of the duplicity and their own unwitting role in it, coined the phrase *Der Führer schenkt den Juden eine Stadt* (The Führer gives the Jews a town) for the film. This has become its unofficial title over the years, and, for anyone not aware of the reality behind the ironic comment, this term of reference could easily be misunderstood.

Act Six: 'Rewarding' the Actors: The Reality behind the Illusion

In June 1944 the BBC World Service broadcast an overt report about a huge number of transports from Theresienstadt to Auschwitz. In this broadcast it was stated that the people would be gassed within six months. This was not propaganda – there was nothing staged about this piece of information. The Gestapo also picked up on this report. The Gestapo relied, however, on the 'the fog of war' to detract from any serious attention to the report or political interventions.
Within a few weeks of the International Red Cross visit, and after the film was almost complete, the set was dismantled and the cast removed. The majority were indeed deported to Auschwitz, whilst for Theresienstadt plans were hatched for

the building of gas chambers. Although the International Red Cross had allowed themselves to be fooled by the Nazis' ruse, perhaps precipitating these deportations, their protestations did succeed in stopping the building of gas chambers also at Theresienstadt.

Gerron, the enthusiastic director of the film and, ultimately, the key player in the making of the deception, was also not spared Auschwitz.

Acknowledgments

I wish to thank staff at the following archives which I visited from 2000 onwards:
Terezin, Czech Republic; International Red Cross, Geneva; Wiener Library, London; Imperial War Museum, London; Academy of Arts, Berlin; and Yad Vashem, Israel.
It was whilst working on documents for a different project at archives in 2002 that I first stumbled upon a reference to some of Shakespeare's plays juxtaposed with Goethe's *Faust* in Theresienstadt, and which inspired this novella, and its title.
I also wish to acknowledge the following source materials which have been used for direct and indirect quotations (at times, slightly adapted by the protagonists for their own purposes):

The Arden Shakespeare Complete Works, 1998 (2001), ed. By Richard Proudfoot, Ann Thompson and David Scott Kastan.

Faust: A Tragedy, by Johann Wolfgang von Goethe. Translated, in the original metres, by Bayard Taylor (late 19th century copy).

A Pocket Guide to Shakespeare's Plays, Kenneth McLeish and Stephen Unwin, 1998 (for part of the dialogue between the main protagonists about Shakespeare's *Merchant of Venice*).

Shakespeare's Advice to the Players, Peter Hall, 2003 (pp.91-93 for part of the final dialogue between the main protagonists).

Hamlet und Deutschland: Zur literarischen Shakespeare-Rezeption im 20. Jahrhundert, Franz Loquai, 1993 (for the affinity of Germany to the figure of Hamlet, and for the way in which Goethe's (misconstrued) comments about Hamlet contributed to this trend).

At the Mind's Limit, Jean Améry, p.40 ('only through torture did he [the tortured person] learn that a living person can be transformed so thoroughly into flesh and by that, while still alive, be partly made into a prey of death')

Four Quartets. Burnt Norton. East Coker. The Dry Salvages. Little Gidding, T.S. Eliot (first published 1944), 1986, p.47.

Furthermore, José Saramago's novel, *Blindness*, also inspired the style of punctuation for this poetic novella.

Author's Personal Comments

This work has evolved over many years. Its origins date back to the period when I was exploring the role of artists and art during the turbulent years of the Weimar Republic (1919-1933). I was fascinated by the artistic and creative synergy of the literary cabarets which brought together high quality artists (new and established) from the fields of music, literature, visual arts and dance. But I was also interested in the immediacy and topicality of the political-literary cabarets which also tried to address the rise of National Socialism through various modes of humour.

In 2000, I realised that I needed to explore beyond the Weimar Republic in order to connect with the fates of individual artists, in spite of the fact that I had not really wanted to get too involved in one of the bleakest periods of history and of humanity: the Third Reich with its manufactured state of fear and terror; with its racially-driven and expansionist policies of 'property-grabbing' and 'land-grabbing'; with its arbitrary justice and executions; and with its mass killings and extermination programmes.

Theresienstadt seemed an obvious place to start this quest. By 2002, I knew that I had to write a play about Theresienstadt – the conference papers I was giving during this period already show these thoughts in action. I made many beginnings – false ones – as they all began with the place. Yet, I knew I wanted to create something which would also transcend time and place, and which would bring humanity, creativity and glimpses of humour to the foreground, in spite of the backdrop. Then suddenly, from nowhere, the two main fictitious protagonists, Carl and Carl's friend began a dramatic dialogue in my mind. It was their individual lives which suddenly spoke to me, which suddenly took hold of me. It was autumn 2004 and I was on a short research-related visit to Berlin. I spent the whole day transcribing their dialogue. I have made only minor changes to this initial impulse which became the foundation for the poetic novella and play.